P9-DHK-959

And we know that all things work together for good
to them that love God, to them who are the called
according to his purpose.
–*Romans* 8:28

This book is dedicated to Phil and Nancy Fay,
horse lovers, baseball fans and faithful servants.

ONE

Barrett Thorn shouted to his younger brother between the clashes of thunder that ripped through the winter darkness. "Gonna go after her. See to the paddock." Swanny, the runaway pregnant mare, was prone to panicking during lightning storms and, true to form, she'd broken through the paddock and bolted.

A flash of lightning illuminated Jack, sitting astride his mare, shoulders hunched against the storm. Barrett was relieved that it was not Jack's twin, Owen, out in the treacherous night. Owen was not physically healed yet, in spite of his bravado. The war had damaged him inside and out. It would be his first Christmas back home since his return from Afghanistan.

In his typical quiet way, Jack didn't answer, pulling his horse into a fluid turn and trotting away through the pouring rain. Their father, Tom, was back at the house where Keegan and Owen were helping him check on the other sixty horses in their care. The Gold Bar Ranch, was the finest setup in the town of Gold Bar and maybe in the entire region, in his humble opinion, but it took all of them to keep it that way. Most of their herd would be fine, Barrett figured, but the more recent arrivals they were boarding for clients over the Christmas holidays might not feel as comfortable in their newer surroundings. Horses could be almost as unpredictable as people. Almost.

From his vantage point on the bluff astride his rock-solid horse, Titan, Barrett had seen only the streak of Swanny's white flanks moving through the undulating branches of the wind-whipped pines. He held Titan still, listening, rain collecting on his close-cut beard and funneling off his hat.

With a section of fencing failing yet again on the western perimeter of the Gold Bar's thousand-acre ranch, the horse would have had easy access to the abutting land, a swath of ravine and hills cut through by a river swollen by yet another storm.

"Why couldn't you stay in the stable like all the other horses?" He was suddenly struck by a memory so strong it hitched up his breath.

"Swanny doesn't care about all your cowboy orders," Sabrina used to say. He could picture his wife, whom he'd nicknamed Bree, so clearly in his mind. Her fringe of blond bangs fell over eyes that saw through his macho facade and right into the most tender places in his soul. Bree was the woman God

"What just happened?" Shelby demanded.

"Dynamite."

She gave Barrett an incredulous look. "Dynamite? As in TNT?"

He nodded. "Plenty left around here from the mining days."

"Why would someone light up a stick and toss it at me? It has to be the guy who threatened me."

"Maybe, unless you've angered somebody else."

She folded her arms and skewered him with such a look of disdain it almost made him smile.

Whatever she had or hadn't done, it wasn't his business. Yet once again, he found himself trying to extricate her from a pile of trouble.

"What makes you think it's not the man who threatened me?" she said.

"Doesn't seem like a rational thing for him to do."

"He threatened to kill me recently, if you remember."

"Words don't mean much. My father believes him to be an honorable man, deep down."

She met his eyes, her own glimmering with unreadable emotion. "I admire that kind of familial respect."

Something was under those words, something deep and painful and raw.

Dana Mentink is an award-winning author of Christian fiction. Her novel *Betrayal in the Badlands* won a 2010 RT Reviewers' Choice Best Book Award, and she was pleased to win the 2013 Carol Award for *Lost Legacy*. She has authored more than a dozen Love Inspired Suspense novels. Dana loves feedback from her readers. Contact her via her website at danamentink.com.

Books by Dana Mentink

Love Inspired Suspense

Gold Coast Cowboys
Cowboy Christmas Guardian

Pacific Coast Private Eyes

Dangerous Tidings
Seaside Secrets
Abducted
Dangerous Testimony

Rookie K-9 Unit

Seek and Find

Wings of Danger

Hazardous Homecoming
Secret Refuge

Stormswept

Shock Wave
Force of Nature
Flood Zone

Visit the Author Profile page at Harlequin.com for more titles.

COWBOY
CHRISTMAS
GUARDIAN

DANA MENTINK

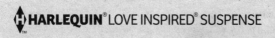

HARLEQUIN® LOVE INSPIRED® SUSPENSE

LOVE INSPIRED BOOKS

Recycling programs for this product may not exist in your area.

ISBN-13: 978-0-373-67860-0

Cowboy Christmas Guardian

Copyright © 2017 by Dana Mentink

www.Harlequin.com

Printed in U.S.A.

meant to be his partner, his love, his best friend, riding beside him through this life.

Except that she was gone in a moment of carelessness, lost in a crushing tangle of metal.

His stomach tensed with white-hot rage at the person who had taken her away and stripped him of any kind of a future.

Titan's uneasy shifting pulled him from the memory. He had to get to Swanny soon, before she broke a leg or got tangled up in barbed wire. He urged Titan through the gap in the busted fence and onto Joe Hatcher's property with only a small flicker of unease.

He wondered if the surly saddler had followed through on his threat to set booby traps to keep local kids from fooling around, searching for gold. If he had the time, he'd knock on Hatcher's door and ask permission, but Swanny was in danger. He wasn't about to let pleasantries get in the way of rescuing the poor beast.

"Hope we don't get shot," he muttered to Titan. They picked their way carefully over the flattest stretch of ground that sloped down to a densely wooded area. Not the greatest place to hang out during a lightning storm, but Swanny was scared, no doubt, and might have headed for the comfort of the overhanging branches.

Barrett rode closer, the noise of the rain mingling with the sound of the swollen river at the bottom of a crevasse just beyond the trees. Fingers to his lips, he let out a piercing whistle which usually alerted his horses that there would be a sugar cube or an apple for them if they presented themselves. It worked on some horses and not on others. Swanny never failed to come for her bit of dessert.

"A hopeless sweet tooth," Bree used to say.

Ducking as the wet branches slapped the back of his neck, he pushed on into the trees. Titan stopped short, as surprised as Barrett at what they saw.

A cream-colored compact car, foreign made, was parked under the bushes. It looked to be fairly new and sported out-of-state Nevada plates. Definitely not a vehicle he'd ever be caught dead in. He could not picture Joe Hatcher driving such a thing either, but who would trespass on his property and go so far as to park their car in such an isolated corner? And for what purpose?

A crackle of branches drew his attention.

"It's Barrett Thorn. I'm looking for my horse," he called out, figuring it was the best way not to get shot if Joe Hatcher was out patrolling his property. "Who's there?"

No answer, but neither did he hear the sound of a shotgun being cocked, so that was a plus.

The rain pounded harder. Titan shifted his weight to indicate that he did not understand his master's crazy choice to remain in the elements when there was a perfectly good barn back on the Gold Bar Ranch.

At the moment, Barrett was beginning to question his own actions, too. Swanny would wind up back at the barn sooner or later, and it would be a lot easier trying to find her after sunup. He might be risking his own safety and that of Titan by continuing the search mission. Was he going the extra mile to find the horse because she was his duty? Or because she had been Bree's favorite?

"You'd do it for any of the horses," he mumbled to himself. He patted Titan's neck, the storm howling around them.

No one emerged from the undergrowth. It must have been an animal or a storm-related noise he'd heard. Of course. What else would it have been? Swanny would have responded to his whistle long ago.

Still, he waited a minute longer. His cowboy hat was not enough to keep the driving rain from snaking down his neck, wetting his shirt under his jacket. His jeans were soaked from his belt to the top of his boots.

If Swanny was in the woods somewhere, she'd have shown herself by now, he felt certain. It was time to search elsewhere. The car would remain a mystery for someone else to solve.

"We'll go check the east end again, in case your daffy girl changed her mind and started back home," he said. Titan twitched an ear, eager to be heading out of the storm, and began his about-face.

Thump.

Barrett pulled Titan to a stop. What he'd heard this time wasn't a twig snapping.

Thump, thump.

Cold prickles erupted on the back of his neck at the sound. Hopping from the saddle, he approached the car.

Another thump and a woman's cry.

Coming from inside the trunk.

Shelby Arroyo slammed her sneakers against the metal lid of the trunk and kicked for all she was worth. The effort sent pain shooting up her neck to her skull where her attacker had struck her from behind while she'd been fumbling in her trunk. She was scared, terrified even and angry at herself.

"How stupid you are," Shelby hissed. "Staying out until nightfall without even letting Uncle Ken know your route." Absorbed in the area geology as she usually was, completely oblivious, she'd not got even a glimpse of the person who had hit her over the head and pushed her in. And where was her cell phone? She stopped kicking long enough to grope again around the pitch-black space, encountering nothing but the bag of extra shoes she'd left there. The little pack she carried with her assaying tools, driver's license, phone, keys and wallet had fallen from her hand, probably taken by her attacker along with her soil samples.

Why? The samples were worthless, just a way for

her to collect information about the area geology, and she had less than twenty dollars in her wallet.

Whoever had done it must have been watching her, biding their time. The thought froze her. Strange hands had lifted her up, dumped her in and left her there. She was fortunate the guy hadn't decided to kill her, unless he figured she'd die in the trunk before anyone found her. It would be a slow, unkind death, of hunger and thirst. A flood of panic stampeded inside. *Stop it, Shelby.*

She kicked again in frustration. "Let…me…out," she hollered to no one. Try as she might, she could find no internal trunk release. There had to be one somewhere, but her shaking fingers simply could not locate it and of course she'd never taken the time to read the owner's manual. *Who imagines they're going to get locked in their own trunk?* she thought bitterly.

The car jolted.

She almost screamed.

Someone was attempting to open the trunk from the outside. Her heart jumped to her throat. Was it help? But who would know where to find her except the man who had locked her there in the first place? No innocent bystander would be out strolling along in a downpour at ten o'clock at night.

He'd come back.

Her mind scrambled, trying to figure out some means of defense. She had nothing, no weapon, no phone. "God…" she started, but that wouldn't do any good. Prayers were fine and all, but she knew she had to rely on herself, as she'd told her mother so many times before the woman no longer knew who Shelby was.

Resolve hardened inside Shelby like hot lava hitting cold ocean water. She intended to use every shred of muscle she possessed to save herself. No divine intervention required. Tensing her legs, she poised to kick out, straining to hear over the whoosh of rain.

Was that footsteps now, heading away?

No. The car was lurching under a heavy onslaught at the front end, the metal shuddering around her. There was a sound of breaking glass. After a moment, the trunk release triggered and the lid slid open a couple of inches. She paused to give him just enough time to return to the back of the vehicle. Timing would be crucial.

One chance is all you get, Shelby, she thought.

She was blinded by the glare from a flashlight whoever it was must have been holding. Another half second. With an explosive effort, she bucked her feet out as hard as she could. The trunk lid made contact.

She heard a man's grunt of surprise and pain, but she did not stop long enough to assess the damage. Instead she was out and running as fast as she could over the open ground.

"Stop," a man's deep voice called.

No way, her mind shot back but her feet did not

slow. Pain pounded through her neck and shoulders but the adrenaline kept it at bay. She had to get to a house or find a place to hole up until morning to buy herself time.

"Stop," the voice came again louder, closer. "There's a…"

She did not hear the last word. Running faster than she'd known she could, Shelby flew, feet slipping on wet rocks and tripping over the uneven patches of ground.

He was drawing nearer, moving surprisingly fast for a big man. A glance told her he was as wet as she was, a cowboy hat hiding his face.

She pressed harder and he yelled again, but she gave his words no heed.

A smell of sodden vegetation and the faraway sound of running water triggered an alarm bell in her mind. Cold air wafted up from somewhere far below. The ground suddenly gave way underneath her as she plunged into nothingness.

TWO

Barrett skidded to a stop at the edge of the ravine, flopping down on his belly. Rain slashed at him and the almost-perfect darkness obliterated her from view. He shined his flashlight down into the ravine.

It took him several minutes to spot her, the gleam of one pale arm showing against the slick rock. She lay perfectly still on her back on a narrow ledge of rock, one leg dangling down into the abyss.

Dead? His blood went cold. *No, not dead, unconscious*, he told himself firmly.

It wasn't going to be easy logistically to get to her. Plus, if she awakened, she'd probably try to claw his eyes out or something and send them both to the bottom of the ravine. Rubbing his chin where the trunk lid had caught him, he tasted blood in his mouth.

He pulled his phone from his pocket, dialed Jack and explained the situation in twenty words or less. Jack would alert their father and brothers. There was no sense contacting the volunteer fire department since it might take upward of thirty minutes to an hour to assemble any kind of rescue group out here, especially on such a night.

Titan eased close at Barrett's whistle. Barrett retrieved a rope from the saddlebag, shoving his hat inside. He tied the rope to a sturdy trunk that overhung the ravine. If he'd stopped to think a minute, he might have considered the recklessness of his actions. Slippery slope, inadequate light, storm raging and a volatile woman at the bottom of it all.

Best to call in rescue and wait, or delay until his brothers showed up. But something in the way she lay there, body twisted, slender and vulnerable in the storm, would not let him delay a moment more.

Looping the other end of the rope around himself, he eased outward into the gap back first, beginning his rappel over the edge.

Titan shook his mane and stamped a hoof on the ground.

"I know, buddy," Barrett muttered. "This is just all kinds of crazy." His horse's brown eyes were the last thing he saw as he plunged into the darkness.

The series of storms had saturated the ground, washing away ribbons of soil and leaving behind a lattice of twisted roots. Bits of rock pattered down from above, striking his neck and shoulders. The rope scratched against his palms, reminding him that he should have had the good sense to retrieve his leather gloves from the saddlebag along with the rope. His boots scraped even more material away from the cliff wall as he navigated down to the ledge.

As far as he could tell, the woman had not moved. The fall hadn't covered a great distance, no more than fifteen feet, he figured, but who knew what kind of injuries she might have sustained if nothing had broken her fall? Again the cold, sick sensation gathered in his belly.

When he was about a yard from the ledge, he stopped, feet braced against the mud. "Ma'am?" he called. "My name is Barrett Thorn and I'm coming to help you."

She didn't answer. He hadn't figured she would, but it was worth a shot.

He settled gingerly onto the ledge, crouching next to her. A mass of wet hair covered her face and he reached out a finger to pull it away. Her profile was visible, nose small, chin narrow, face heart shaped. The delicacy of it struck him.

Without warning, he was plunged back in time some four years earlier, when he'd pulled Bree from the wrecked car. Her eyes had been shut, too, but they'd fluttered open for one precious moment before they'd closed for the last time. There was nothing in this world that could hurt worse than that, except being reminded every day in a million ways that he was alone. Strange the things he missed about Bree.

The pillow next to his with a satin case to "keep

away the wrinkles" of which he'd never seen a hint on her face.

Her ready laughter.

The smell of the candles she always insisted on lighting for every evening meal.

Her horrendous cooking. He even missed that. What he wouldn't give for a chance to eat another plateful of tuna casserole, crunchy with half-cooked noodles. He swatted at a trail of water running down his cheek. *Business at hand, Barrett.*

Swallowing hard, he found the junction of the unconscious woman's chin and neck, and pressed his fingers there, seeking a pulse.

"Lord God," he prayed, but he could not finish. The last time he had prayed for the life of a young woman, his woman, his love, God's answer had been no. Gritted teeth, pounding heart, his soul quaked with fear that he would find no spark of life. Gone, like Bree, with him crouched there helpless. Rubbing his hands as dry as he could, he tried one more time. This time, the proof was dramatic.

She jerked to a sitting position with a scream and shot out a hand that nearly shoved him over the edge.

"Easy," he said, holding open palms up to show her he was not a threat. "I'm not going to hurt you."

Her eyes were wide as silver dollars, whole body trembling. Her breath came in short bursts as she scrabbled away as far as she could get from him. He attempted to reassure her that he wasn't some random killer who'd appeared on a ledge in a storm, but she moved backward and he lunged forward to catch her.

The rock ledge gave way beneath her feet. Her eyes were bright with fear as she disappeared before his eyes for the second time.

Shelby's senses cartwheeled through a dizzying cascade as her legs slithered over the side. Pitch-black night, cold rain, the sick sensation of no ground under her feet. The jagged edge of rocks cut into her belly as she clutched at anything that might keep her from falling the rest of the way.

"Help," she wanted to scream, but she could not manage a single syllable as she continued to slip down the slope.

Rocks ground against her hips and roots broke away under her fingers. She felt a jerk and a painful pressure on her wrist. Looking up against the sheeting rain, she saw the man with the beard hanging on to her wrist with both hands. His full mouth was contorted with the effort.

No, no, her mind screamed. He'd come to finish what he'd started when he'd struck her and stuffed her in the trunk of her car. She braced her legs against the canyon wall to push away.

"Listen," he said between clenched teeth. "I am not the guy who hurt you. You're just gonna have to trust me on that because you're wiggling and I don't wanna drop you."

Trust him? She had no intention of doing any such thing, but the canyon below her did not give her much choice. Die on the rocks, or live long enough to get away from the bearded guy? Her forearms ached and her ribs burned with pain.

"Give me your other hand," he ordered.

Fighting her instincts, she heaved her other arm up and he clasped it tight. They both breathed hard for a few seconds before he began to haul her back up. She helped with her legs as much as she could. Inch by painful inch, she was pulled upward until she landed on her knees on the ledge. The man bent over at the waist, panting.

Their eyes locked, like two wild animals sizing each other up.

"Barrett," came a shout from above, making her jump.

"I got her," he hollered back. "Gonna need to pull us up."

There was some response that she could not decipher.

He puffed out a breath and straightened, rising to something over six feet she guessed, plenty strong enough to have clobbered her and shoved her into the trunk. Then again, if his goal was to hurt her, why would he have kept her from falling into the ravine? Doubt clouded her thinking along with the cold that seemed to be freezing her one layer at a time.

"All right," he said. "My brothers are going to

pull us up on the rope, so you have to hang on to me for a minute, okay?"

Not okay. The furthest thing from okay. To deliver herself into the hands of this stranger and now his brothers? Needing more time to think, she shook her head.

His expression went a little softer, or so she imagined. "I know you've been through a fright and you're scared, but I'm a good guy, mostly." He offered a wry smile. "At least, some folks might say so. I'm not here to hurt you, but there's really no way I can prove that to you under the present circumstances."

He could be telling the truth but her fear still ran rampant. She pressed herself to the cliff wall, staying far out of reach.

He tucked his hands onto his hips. "All right. If that's your choice, we'll honor it. I've never in my life forced a woman to do anything she didn't want to, but I for one am tired of being out here in the rain, and I've got a horse to find, so if you really want to stay down here by yourself, it's a long wait until sunrise."

She saw now there was a rope knotted around his waist. He looped an extra length around himself, grabbed hold above his head and shouted to his brothers to start pulling.

Below, the river water rushed wildly on past the rocky ground. The wind teased her wet skin, her body shivering uncontrollably. She recalled her mother's admonition, always gentle, too gentle. *So stubborn, Shell. It's not always you against the world.*

"Wait," she said.

Water ran down his crew-cut hair and wide chin. Slowly he held out a hand to her.

Just get out of the ravine, she told herself. *Then you can figure if this guy is the genial cowboy or the man who locked you up.* She reached out shaking fingers. His palms were rough and calloused, the hands of a working man, and he scooped her to his side in one strong movement.

His shoulders were solid, wide under the sodden jacket, his waist tapered and trim as she clung to him, gripping his leather belt.

"Keep holding on tight," he advised.

She did as the rope was pulled up from above. The journey threatened to spin them in circles, but the man she'd heard called Barrett kept them relatively steady by bracing his long legs against the canyon walls.

Foot by slippery foot, they gradually reached the top where she found herself surrounded by three more men and their horses. Their physical similarities marked them as brothers, except for the one who was more slender and lanky than the other three.

"I'll call for an ambulance when I can get a signal," said the brother who was still astride his horse. He peered down at her curiously.

Another handed her a blanket. Barrett helped wrap it around her shoulders.

"Mama's waiting at the house," one of the brothers said.

Barrett nodded, taking the reins to a big horse from one and retrieving his wet hat from the saddlebag. "You can ride with me—" he hesitated "—unless you'd rather not."

She was miserable and shivering badly as she surveyed the men who stared at her. Something in their appearance took the edge off her suspicion, or maybe it was the reference to Mama. She'd always called her mother that, a sweet endearment that bridged the gap between angry daughter and desperate mother. *Mama.* Two syllables packed to the brim with feelings, and she would give anything to say it one more time and see understanding in her mother's eyes.

We're oil and water sometimes, Shelby, but I'll always be your Mama.

Oil and water. More like fire and ice.

Mama, I miss you.

Expelling a breath and straightening her shoulders, she nodded. Barrett got onto his horse in one fluid motion and offered her an arm.

After a moment of paralyzing doubt, she took it and he swung her up behind him.

"Where are we going?" she said into his ear.

"Home," he said, urging the horse through the pounding rain.

THREE

Barrett was not too cold to feel uncomfortable at having a woman's arms wrapped around his waist. It had been four long years since any woman had touched him except his mother and assorted relatives. The lady was strong and soft at the same time, holding on to him tentatively, it seemed to him. Fortunately, Titan was eager to get back to the barn so his pace was brisk as they returned to the house.

The string of Christmas lights twined around the porch railing twinkled in the gloom. His father met them, taking the reins from Barrett as he helped the woman off the horse. Barrett tied the horses under the wide porch as a temporary measure until he could unsaddle them, dry them down and see to their feed.

His father tipped his wet hat to her and introduced himself. "Tom Thorn. Very sorry for your trouble, miss. Come inside and my wife, Evie, will help you feel comfortable."

"Thank you," she said.

"Got Swanny," he said to Barrett. "She's in the barn, looking plenty sorry."

"I'm sure." Barrett chuckled. More likely, she was pleased as could be now that she was back in a warm stable with a bucket of oats. It eased his mind to know that his wife's dotty horse was unhurt after her mad escape.

Barrett's mother stood in the doorway, gesturing. "Enough chatting, Barrett. Bring that poor girl in the house."

"Yes, ma'am." He followed her in where Evie looked the woman up and down. His mother was all of four feet eleven inches, hair graying but green eyes sparkling as brightly as they ever had.

"What's your name, honey?" she asked.

"Shelby," the woman replied, teeth chattering.

"Well, Miss Shelby, I am eager to hear how in the world you got halfway down a ravine on Joe Hatcher's property, but first things first. Everybody needs some dry clothes. I've got a pot of coffee on, so go change, boys, and we'll have a talk."

She put an arm around Shelby's shoulders. "Come with me. We'll get you a change of clothes and check out your bruises." She chuckled. "Don't worry. I was an RN before I traded it in for ranch life, so I'm not just a nosy mom to those four gorillas."

Barrett marched to his room, stripped off his wet clothes and pulled on a dry pair of jeans and a T-shirt, along with his less favored pair of boots. He tried not to rush, but he was dying to hear Shelby's story. It was an odd sensation. Since Bree died, he had been interested in nothing and no one, only his family and the workings of the Gold Bar Ranch where his life was 100 percent about the horses.

Forcing a slow pace, he ambled into the kitchen to find twins, Jack and Owen, sitting at the table sipping coffee while their youngest brother, Keegan, leaned against the refrigerator, munching a cheese sandwich.

Keegan had a bottomless appetite and a head for mischief. He shook his dark hair from his face and grinned. "So, Barrett. For once it's not me that broke the rules. What's it feel like to be a trespasser?"

Owen laughed as their father joined them. "Good thing you didn't run across any of Joe Hatcher's booby traps."

"Those are rumors," their father said with a frown. He scrubbed a hand over a scalp of stubbly gray hair that had not thinned in spite of his seventy-three years. "Joe is a good man, or used to be. Top-notch saddler until his life took a turn."

"If you say so," Owen said.

"I do say so, son," he said quietly. "Everyone's life takes a turn now and then, doesn't it?"

"Yes, sir." Owen looked at the table, probably feeling again the enemy bullets that had carved a trail into his leg and left him scarred and limping. Keegan understood, too. He was adopted into the Thorn family at age sixteen when there was no one to care for him but Evie and Tom Thorn. In Barrett's case, one careless turn of a drunk driver's wheel had brought his life to a full stop.

Yes, he agreed. Life could take a sudden turn.

Owen and Jack stood as their mother ushered Shelby in and seated her in one of their vacated chairs.

At last he could get a good look at her. Trying not to stare, he drank in the details. She was slender and fine boned, probably somewhere close to five feet seven inches. Now he could see that her eyes were the green of forest moss, her hair brown. She'd pulled it into a wet ponytail that swept the flannel shirt his mom had loaned her. A navy blue pair of sweatpants, which his mother must have dug up from somewhere, engulfed her legs.

"I think she's going to be okay," Evie said. "But I would lobby for a hospital visit to be sure there isn't a concussion from where she was struck on the head."

Struck on the head? What kind of person would hit a woman? That notion made his stomach flip. And the fact that she thought he'd done it? He cleared his throat and introduced everyone properly.

Shelby nodded solemnly at each brother and his parents.

"Thank you," she said, her gaze finally landing on him. "Especially you, Barrett. I… I thought…"

She twisted a finger in the hem of her borrowed shirt. "Well, anyway, thank you."

He nodded. "What were you doing on Hatcher's property?"

His mother shot him a scolding look. "Can you offer her a cup of coffee before you start the interrogation? Even cowboys should have good manners."

Ignoring the smiles from his brothers, he poured a cup of coffee and handed it to Shelby.

"Thank you," she said, the slight quirk of her lips indicating she was enjoying seeing him chastised. "I thought I was still on my uncle's property. I got caught up in my work and I didn't realize I'd strayed. Lost track of the time, too." She looked thoroughly embarrassed.

Her uncle? Which of their neighbors was her relation? He was about to ask when a loud pounding on the front door made her jump, spilling some of the coffee.

"Don't think that's the cops yet," Owen said. "I called them, but they're working an overturned lumber truck on the main road that has traffic stopped in and out of town." He opened the door.

Joe Hatcher stepped in, white hair plastered over his skull. His angry gaze swept the kitchen until it fastened on Shelby. "I was out checking my property. Saw Barrett pulling you out of the ravine. You got no business on my land, like I told you last week. You trespass again and you're gonna get hurt," he snarled.

All the brothers stepped a pace forward.

"You'll be civil," their father said, "or you'll leave."

"Civil?" Hatcher's eyes narrowed. "I gotta be civil when she can trespass on my land? Go poking around in my mine?"

"I wasn't anywhere near your mine and I didn't mean to stray onto your property. That was my mistake. I was taking some samples along the road and I got disoriented."

Samples? For what purpose? Barrett wondered.

"Fool thing to do. You deserve what you got," Hatcher said.

Shelby stood and lifted her chin. "So was it you who hit me from behind and locked me in the trunk of my car?"

"'Course not," he said. "If I'd known you were on my land, I'd have shot you."

Evie gasped and Barrett started to speak, but Shelby faced Hatcher, a glint of fire in her expression. "There is no need for threats. I apologize for trespassing. I was taking some surface samples and I didn't realize I was no longer on my uncle's property."

"But let's be clear," she continued. "That isn't your mine. I have every right to enter and collect samples and I will do that in the near future."

"You gonna tell me I don't own the property

that's been in my family for a hundred years?" he snapped.

"Of course you own the land. That's why I came to see you last week, but you wouldn't talk to me. As I would have explained if you'd answered your phone or read your mail, you don't own the mineral rights. My uncle does, and he wants an assay of the ore. That's my job and you don't have the legal right to interfere."

Hatcher's mouth worked, brows drawn into a ferocious scowl. "I don't care what the law says. If you step on my property again, I'll kill you."

Barrett's pulse hammered as he grabbed Hatcher by the arm. "That's enough. You're leaving."

Hatcher shook away Barrett's grip but stalked to the front door with Barrett following. "Get your car off my property," he called to Shelby. Before he stepped outside, he poked Barrett in the chest. "You won't be so eager to help when you know who her kin is," he hissed.

Barrett stared him down. "Doesn't matter. You're not going to come into this home and threaten a woman's life."

Muttering, Hatcher stomped down the porch steps.

Barrett shut the door, Hatcher's words replaying in his mind. As he returned to the kitchen, a trickle of suspicion slithered through his belly. It couldn't be. "Shelby, who is your uncle?"

"Ken Arroyo," she said. "Do you know him?"

Barrett could feel the weight of his family staring at him. Time seemed to slow as if the hands of the old carriage clock were being held by some invisible force, his breaths ticking along in rhythm.

"Yes," he said finally. "I know him."

"You're neighbors," she said uncertainly, "even though he's not here for part of the year. You must be friends, then?"

"No, not friends." *The furthest thing from friends.*

She cocked her head slightly, long tendrils that had escaped the ponytail curling around her face, her glance taking in the stricken looks around the table. "I can see that my uncle has no fans here. Do you want to tell me what's going on?"

No, he thought. *No, I don't.*

She watched Barrett exhale long and slow. He couldn't be older than his early thirties but there was a deep storehouse of grief and fatigue in his electric-blue eyes that made her wonder. He rubbed a hand over his chin as if to smooth away some painful thought.

"Not the time. If you're feeling better, I'll drive you to the hospital, or you're welcome to wait here for the police."

"I don't need a hospital. I need to get back. The police can talk to me at Uncle Ken's house." She stood. "I'm okay and I can find my own way to my car."

"Begging your pardon, but I'll escort you."

"Not necessary."

Barrett didn't answer.

Evie appeared to have recovered her composure. "We will bring you your clothes when they're dry."

"Thank you very much, but I can pick them up. You have all been extremely kind. I can't thank you enough."

Evie took her by the hand. There was something forced in her smile and it made Shelby sad. For a few minutes, it had been nice to feel like someone's daughter again. It pained her that somehow things had changed, though she didn't know why.

"That's what neighbors do," Evie said. "Barrett will see you back."

Barrett stood stiffly by the door.

"Hey," Owen said, moving close to his brother. Shelby noted he had a pronounced limp. "I can take her," he said quietly, but Shelby heard him anyway.

Barrett shook his head. "I got this."

What was it about her relationship with Uncle Ken that had instantaneously set up a wall between her and the Thorn family?

It's not your problem. You're here for Uncle Ken. The Thorns could put up walls for whatever reason and it was of no consequence to her. At the moment, her entire life goal was to get back to her uncle's place and enjoy the hottest shower she could stand.

Barrett led her outside. As she passed the foyer, she caught the scent of pine from a Christmas tree. It was standing in the corner of the room, festooned with ornaments. On the fireplace mantel, green branches were trimmed with tiny red glass balls. A framed photo graced the mantel, a grinning Barrett without the cowboy hat, his arm around a young woman, radiant in a wedding dress, her long hair pinned back with white roses. She was lovely. Barrett flicked her a glance, catching Shelby looking at the picture. She looked away and followed him outside.

The rain had slackened off to a weak sprinkle. The events of the day overwhelmed her as her mind spooled through the memories. A sudden blow to the head, the sensation of being hauled into her trunk, the awful sound of the lid slamming shut.

The attack had been from Joe Hatcher, she was sure of it, but why? Just to keep her away from the mine? Out of greed? Anger at her perceived trespassing? Or perhaps he had some deep-seated resentment about her uncle, too?

"You ride?" Barrett said, pulling her back to the present.

"Since I was a kid," she said. That was probably overstating. She'd slacked off on her riding since her youth when she would visit her uncle in the summertime, but she found herself wanting to prove her worth to Barrett Thorn. Bad enough that he'd had to rescue her from a locked trunk and lug her out of a ravine. She couldn't leave him thinking she was some flimsy damsel-in-distress type.

He untied the horse that Jack had been riding. "Lady is a gentle ride."

She was right. He did think she was clueless. Ignoring his offered hand, she put her foot in the stirrup and climbed onto the saddle.

Barrett mounted his horse and clicked his tongue at the big animal.

Shelby was grateful that the rain had tapered off. Moonlight cast a weak glow over the landscape as they trailed back to where she'd parked her car. Her own stupid mistake made her groan inwardly. Some assayer. Hadn't even realized she'd strayed onto Hatcher's property.

Determined not to incur any more embarrassment for one evening, she slipped off Lady and handed the reins to Barrett. He was a giant astride the big horse, and as immovable as a cliff.

"Thank you again," she said. "I owe you a debt of gratitude."

"Don't owe me anything. I'll help you find your keys or maybe I can hot-wire it."

"No need for you to stay. I'll find them."

He ignored her, dismounting and beginning a search of the wet ground.

She hesitated, curiosity burning inside. "Barrett, what do you have against my uncle?"

He looked away. "Don't need to talk about that now."

"It's not likely we're going to do much chatting in the future." That got no reaction. "So tell me. If you have a beef against Uncle Ken, then I have a right to know. He's my only family."

Barrett's mouth tightened into a thin line. "No disrespect intended, ma'am, but you don't have a right to know."

She folded her arms, her pulse kicking up. "If Uncle Ken has an enemy right next door, then it is my business."

Barrett looked down at her, considering, shoulders a broad, tense wall against the night sky. He blew out a breath. "All right. You want to know so bad, I'll tell you."

She waited quietly.

"Ken's son killed my wife."

The words dropped like stones. *Killed my wife.* She found herself unable to speak. An endless moment passed between them but she could not think of a single response.

"Let's find those keys," he finally said.

Her thoughts ran rampant as they searched. Glass littered the ground from where Barrett had broken the window.

Her cousin Devon had killed Barrett Thorn's wife? She flashed back to the photo she'd seen, a radiant bride and her handsome groom. With a surge of guilt, she realized she hadn't been back to her uncle's ranch in so long that she had only known the barest hint about what was going on in the lives of Uncle Ken and Devon.

She'd known Devon had gone to prison for causing an accident that had killed a woman, but she did not know the particulars. The times she'd called, Uncle Ken had steadfastly refused to discuss it.

Still lost in thought, she found her pack under a nearby shrub. There was no sign of her samples, but everything else was there.

Barrett held the reins of the two horses in his hands. He looked somewhere over her head, anywhere but in her eyes.

"I'll wait until you get your car started," he said. "Good night, Miss Arroyo."

In his tone, she heard the bitterness. *Ken's son killed my wife.* She was anxious to get away, to sort it all out in her mind.

A noise behind her made her turn.

Barrett was staring at something in the distance. His attention was riveted to a spot under the trees, pitch-black except for a soft orange glow.

Her mind was slow to put it together. The orange glow was not an electric or battery light. It sparkled and fizzed like a firecracker on the Fourth of July.

No, not a firecracker.

A fuse.

"No," Barrett shouted.

Shelby could not see who was standing there under the trees. With a blur of movement, the stranger launched the dynamite through the air. It arced a golden trail through the night, speeding straight toward her.

FOUR

Barrett dropped the reins, grabbed Shelby's hand and yanked her after him. There wasn't time to do anything but dive behind a pile of boulders and put his bulk between her and whatever shrapnel was about to come their way.

The explosion was deafening. Shards of glass flew through the air, smashing on the rocks and cutting into his back as he tried to block Shelby from the falling debris. His eardrums rang with the percussive burst. The ground shuddered under them. He looked up in time to see Lady and Titan bolt, fleeing to the safety of the trees.

Shelby stirred in his arms but he caged her there with his body.

"Stay still until we know there's nothing else coming."

She probably wasn't thrilled about his command, but she acquiesced.

It was silent save for the wind in the branches and his own harsh breathing. Through the thin jacket his mother had insisted she wear, he felt her sides rising and falling in rapid rhythm. After a few moments, he poked his head up above the pile of rocks, watching for signs of movement. He saw nothing but a flicker of white as Titan led Lady away from the danger.

Barrett eased up and crawled from the hiding place, offering Shelby a hand. She took it, and together they surveyed the damage. He still kept a cautious eye on the trees.

The front of her car was blackened and twisted, smoke pouring out through the broken windshield. Her expression was hard to read in the scant moonlight. Fear? Outrage? Confusion? All of them would apply.

"What just happened?" she demanded, hands on hips.

"Dynamite."

She gave him an incredulous look. "So somebody actually ignited a stick of dynamite and lobbed it at me?"

He nodded. "Plenty left around here from the mining days. Easy to lay hands on it."

"I don't care where it came from. The bigger point here is why would someone light up a stick and toss it at me? It has to be Joe Hatcher."

"Maybe, unless you've angered somebody else."

She folded her arms and skewered him with such a look of disdain it almost made him smile.

"I haven't done anything to anyone in this town."

He didn't answer. Whatever she had or hadn't done wasn't his business. Yet once again, he found himself trying to extricate her from a pile of trouble.

"What makes you think it's not Joe Hatcher?" she said.

"Doesn't seem like a rational thing for him to do."

"He threatened to kill me recently, if you remember."

"And that was completely out of line, but he might have been shooting his mouth off. My father believes him to be an honorable man, deep down."

"And you believe that, too?"

He cocked his head. "I don't know, but I trust my father. So for now, I'll reserve judgment."

She met his eyes, her own glimmering with unreadable emotion. "I admire that kind of familial respect."

Something was under those words, something deep and painful and raw.

Since he did not know what to say, he dialed his cell phone and told his family about the newest development.

"Road's still blocked to our ranch," Owen told him. "Cops said they'll circle around and meet you at Arroyo's place."

Arroyo's place. He'd rather crawl through a cactus field, but he could not think of any way out of it. "Okay," he said.

"Need backup?"

"Nah, thanks, though."

He pocketed the phone and joined Shelby, who was examining the remains of her car.

"As soon as I get the horses back, we'll go to your uncle's place. Cops will meet us there."

She stared gloomily at the wrecked vehicle. "My first new car."

He decided it was not the time to tell her a nice half-ton pickup might have held up better than her flimsy foreign-made tin can.

His mother's voice rang through his memory. *In the multitude of words there wanteth not sin: but he that refraineth his lips is wise.* He'd had to copy that proverb out as punishment a number of times when he was a kid. All the Thorn brothers had, except Jack, who was so quiet no one ever knew what he was thinking.

And then there was the youngest Thorn. Their mother would probably still be having Keegan write out Bible verses if she could get him to do it. Barrett didn't figure Keegan would ever master the art of restraint.

He heard no sign at all that the person who had tossed the dynamite was still around, so he figured it was okay to leave Shelby there while he went after the horses. Titan wouldn't have gone too far and Lady would stay with him. Horses weren't as smart as humans, but they knew the survival basics.

Retrieving his hat from the ground and shaking off a sprinkling of glass and dirt, he put it on and headed for the trees. He was surprised to find that Shelby was following him.

"I... I figured I'd help," she said.

Help? That surprised him. Maybe she was scared to be left alone, but she seemed like the kind who wasn't scared of much.

A memory came back to him so strong it cut his heart in two. His wife, Bree, was the bravest woman he'd known, but she'd been petrified of snakes. The day a little gopher snake wriggled into the kitchen, she'd leaped onto Barrett's back piggyback-style, hollering for him to get rid of it. He'd been laughing so hard tears had run down his face.

A drop of rain splatted his cheek and he realized he was standing still. Shelby was looking at him inquiringly.

"Are you okay?" she said softly.

"Just thinking." He turned away and she laid her hand very gently on his shoulder.

"Wait a minute. You're bleeding. I think you got cut by some flying glass."

He shrugged. "It's okay."

But she did not let go. Instead she lifted the bottom edge of his jacket. He felt her fingers graze over his back, the sting of the cool air against the cut at odds with the softness of her touch.

"It doesn't look deep, but it needs bandaging."

He was caught there, wanting to pull away, yet part of him wished to stay, to accept the comfort of her gentle fingers, a connection he had not experienced in a very long time. Blinking, he cleared his throat, moving just enough that she let go of his jacket.

"There," he said, relief pouring through him. "There's Titan." He whistled and the horse approached, with Lady following a pace behind. He took the reins and patted the horse. "It's all right, buddy. The dynamite scared all of us."

Lady was composed enough to allow Shelby to mount. When Barrett was astride Titan, they headed along the muddy trail toward Ken Arroyo's property.

He had not spoken to Ken since the trial when Devon was imprisoned for killing Bree. Ken had bought his son the fancy car and given him all the money he needed to enable his party-boy lifestyle. As far as Barrett was concerned, Ken might as well have bought his good-for-nothing son the liquor that he guzzled before getting behind the wheel.

Anger lit inside Barrett's gut like a burning coal, just as hot as it had been since his wife was taken from him.

Would he be able to keep his mouth shut to prevent the ire from spilling out like acid?

Just keep quiet, he told himself as they picked their way toward the house of his enemy.

Shelby was lost in thought as they followed the trail to her uncle's property. Who would want to throw her in the trunk of her car and then toss a stick of dynamite at her? It had to be Joe Hatcher. He had threatened to kill her, hadn't he? But what would he gain except to keep her out of the mine and buy himself a whole lot of unwanted attention?

As they neared the ranch, she could see Barrett straighten. His back must be hurting. Her fingers tingled at the memory of his strong muscles. The man despised her uncle, yet he'd twice bailed her out of a terrible situation. It must be that cowboy-honor thing.

She felt a deep-down ache in her temple behind her left eye. Migraine or a residual pain from her attack? No time to ponder that as the big ranch house loomed before them.

Uncle Ken had built the home thirty years before, as a summer place for him and his wife, Opal, but Opal had died in childbirth.

Uncle Ken lived most of the year on the east coast with Devon, tending to his commercial real estate business and summering at the California ranch until Devon was fifteen. Summers there had been idyllic. The three of them— Shelby, her sister, Erin, and Devon—rode horses, drank lemonade and caught frogs in the creek.

She'd envied Devon for his situation. It was so different from her own, as a child of a single mother who quaked with fear when the monthly bills came due. She wondered how Devon was faring now. State prison was a world removed from his comfortable home with Uncle Ken.

A police car was parked in front of the two-story house on the wide circular drive. Barrett looped the reins around a split rail fence. Uncle Ken was an equine fanatic and he kept three horses in the back pasture even though he rarely rode anymore, leaving their care to an employee, but she figured Barrett wasn't about to make himself or his own horses at home on Uncle Ken's ranch.

His son killed my wife.

She'd not seen Devon since his high school graduation, the happy kid with the wide smile. How differently Barrett must see him, the killer of his wife. She had no idea how the next few minutes would go as she reached the front door. Barrett followed her in, lingering a few paces behind.

The lamps in the front parlor illuminated a well-appointed front room with sleek leather furniture and richly hued area rugs, not a Christmas decoration to be seen anywhere. Uncle Ken was deep in conversation with a young police officer whose close-cropped hair and rain slicker were damp. Her uncle broke off and wrapped Shelby in a hug, his wide face flushed with emotion.

"I can't believe what's happened to you. Are you okay? Are you hurt at all?"

"No," she said, giving him a reassuring squeeze. "I'm okay, thanks to Mr. Thorn."

Barrett grimaced.

Uncle Ken's mouth twitched as he looked at Barrett. "Thank you," he said quietly, "for taking care of my niece."

Barrett shrugged, hands jammed into his pockets, avoiding eye contact. His jaw was tight, shoulders tense.

The police officer introduced himself to Shelby. "I'm Chris Larraby. I'll be handling your case. I spoke to Joe Hatcher. He was upset about the trespassing, but he says he had nothing to do with locking you in your trunk."

"Well, now we've got a stick of dynamite thrown into the mix," Shelby said. "You can ask him about that."

"Did either of you see who threw it?"

Barrett shook his head.

"I didn't see a thing either," Shelby added.

"It had to be Hatcher," Uncle Ken said. "He made threats."

"Doesn't prove anything," Barrett said.

"It's common sense. Why would you defend him?" Ken's eyes narrowed. "Is it because Shelby is my kin? You'd be happy to see her hurt to get back at me, is that it?"

Barrett's eyes blazed. "No, that's not it."

Larraby raised a palm. "Let's leave the past out of it."

Barrett's expression read, "How are we gonna do that?" But he kept quiet.

Shelby went over the details again while Larraby jotted notes on a small pad of paper. He tucked it into his front pocket. "We'll photograph and give it a once over when the storm's through. In the meantime, Miss Arroyo, I'd advise that you don't go poking around Gold Bar by yourself until we figure out what's going on here."

He paused at the door. "And tell your family to keep their cool also, huh, Barrett?"

Barrett's chin went up. "I'm not telling them anything. We have nothing to do with any of this."

"Yeah?" Larraby's voice went so quiet Shelby almost didn't hear it. "If there's trouble around, Keegan's usually not far away."

Barrett's nostrils flared and the vein in his jaw jumped. "Do your job and solve the case, Larraby," he said. "I don't want anything to do with the Arroyos, and neither does my family."

Shelby watched Barrett stalk through the door. Her emotions clashed loudly inside her. So Barrett and his family wanted nothing to do with her? That was just fine, but if Barrett thought she was going to get run out of town on a rail, he had another think coming. She owed everything to her uncle, the man who had financed her college education, tried to help her mother when the creditors came calling. He was practically a parent to her since her mother had denied Shelby and Erin access to their real father, or so she'd believed until recently.

I'm not going to tuck my tail and run, Barrett, she

thought. She would do the job her uncle had hired her to do and nothing, not Joe Hatcher or the Thorn family or anyone else, would stand in her way.

FIVE

At his customary hour of 4:00 a.m., Barrett made it into the kitchen and grabbed a cup of coffee. The cuts on his back stung, but work would make him forget about the discomfort. Owen was already sitting at the table with a steaming mug. He immediately stopped massaging his upper thigh when Barrett arrived, but not quickly enough.

Barrett sat across from him. "Pain bad today?"

Owen shook off the question. "No."

It was not the truth, of course. Barrett could see by the slight sheen of perspiration on his brother's forehead that his leg was killing him. It also meant he was still steering clear of the pain meds that had been more destructive than the bullets. *Stay strong, brother.*

"Checking fences today with Jack. Can you and Keegan handle the feeding?"

"I can handle it myself," Owen said defiantly, challenging his brother to disagree. He did not. Barrett knew the power of work could heal a man; it had helped heal him after Bree's death. Ken Arroyo's words from the night before galled him afresh.

Is it because Shelby is my kin? You'd be happy to see her hurt to get back at me, is that it?

Barrett's bitterness was mixed with shame because, following the accident, he'd been in such anguish, steeped in rage unlike he'd ever experienced, that he'd wished every bad thing he could imagine on the Arroyo family. Years of prayer and penitence and God's grace had helped restore him, at least mostly. He had not found the strength to completely forgive Devon Arroyo yet, but at least the rage no longer completely consumed him from the inside out. Devon was a kid who'd made a tragic mistake. Barrett's feelings for Ken were another matter entirely.

Again the conversation circled through his mind.

I don't want anything to do with the Arroyos, and neither does my family.

Well, that part was true anyway. Shelby Arroyo could solve her own problems.

"That's it?" Owen said.

"That's what?"

"You're not going to talk about what happened last night with you and Shelby?"

"I already told you. It's all over."

Owen raised an eyebrow and chugged some coffee. "You two almost got blown up, and you're not worried about her?"

"She's not my problem, and she can take care of herself."

"Uh-huh. Locked in a trunk and almost blown up in the same day. Clearly she can take care of herself."

Barrett grabbed his jacket, unwilling to talk anymore about Shelby. "Mama wants mistletoe."

Owen laughed. "Of course she does. I'll give that job to Keegan. He climbs trees like a monkey."

Barrett and Jack met up in the stable. Jack had already saddled both Lady and Titan, who seemed to be suffering no ill effects from their frightening episode the evening before.

For a second, Barrett wondered if Shelby had any nightmares about what happened. Bree had periodic nightmares that would leave her trembling and crying. He would roll over and embrace her, kiss her hair and rub circles on her back until she fell asleep again. Funny, she could never recall the bad dreams upon waking.

"You make them go away," she would say, "so I can't remember."

Oh, how he'd loved her. Sometimes he wished he could forget the pain just as easily as she forgot the nightmares. But the pain was a part of the blessing God had given him in Bree, and he would not reject a single moment of it, anguish and all. Bree was with God and she knew no pain, that was his comfort.

He pulled himself back to the present. Jack was

already leading Lady out, so he scrambled to catch up, wondering why his thoughts of Shelby and Bree were getting tangled together.

The fences were in better shape than he anticipated and by lunchtime they were heading back after a few minor fixes. The clouds promised more rain, but for now the sky was holding. He admired the wet gold of the grass which would not regain its brilliant emerald until the spring. The glistening oaks dripped down on them as they picked their way back to the house at just after eleven. His stomach rumbled and the horses were hungry, too, judging by the way they picked up their pace as they neared the barn.

Barrett handed Titan over to Ella Cahill, who beamed a bright smile from under her tangle of red hair. Though she was in her late twenties, she barely came up to the horses' withers. Ella was tiny but ferociously devoted to her disabled sister and to the Thorns, whom she treated as family. She and Owen had been inseparable as young children. She'd got into some trouble after Owen deployed, but Barrett didn't know the particulars.

"Hey, Barrett. You're late. Did you forget Titan is due for his pedicure?"

In spite of her young age, Ella was the best farrier that had ever worked at Gold Bar Ranch. She had a gift, a connection with the horses that defied description. "No way. Didn't forget."

"I'll get Titan some breakfast. He likes to munch while I work on him," she said.

Barrett caught sight of an older horse that gleamed almost white gold, narrow chested with a bright silky mane, delicate and powerful at the same time. He did a double take. "Isn't that Arroyo's Akhal Teke? Is Ken here?"

Ella shook her head, smile dimming. "No, his niece is, and I already got the third degree from Ms. Arroyo so it's your turn. She's in the house," she said, turning away to lead Titan into the barn.

"The third degree about what?" Barrett called to her, but she didn't answer.

He stared from the high-spirited horse, which was eyeing him suspiciously, to the house. What was Shelby Arroyo doing back at the Gold Bar? And what was she doing riding a hot-blooded horse like the Akhal Teke?

Jack fisted his hands on his hips. "You coming?"

Barrett suddenly felt unsure, reluctant to subject himself to Shelby's soft green eyes. He felt like bolting as Titan had done to escape the dynamite. Why the sudden onslaught of ridiculous emotion? What was the matter with him?

"Yeah, I'm coming," he said angrily, cramming his hat more firmly on his head as he strode past his brother.

Shelby held her chin up as she heard the noise from outside. Barrett's mother stood and went to the big simmering pot on the stove.

"Boys will want some soup on a cold day like

this," Evie said. "They've been up since before sunrise checking fences."

Shelby had been hoping she'd somehow miss seeing one particular Thorn brother. All she'd needed was her pile of clothes and some information, which she'd been semisuccessful in prying out of the farrier. "I'll get out of your way. Thank you for laundering my clothes, Mrs. Thorn."

"Please call me Evie. Why don't you stay for lunch? I'm baking gingerbread men later and I'd love some help. The boys are terrible at decorating cookies. My gingerbread men all turn out looking like zombies after the boys are done."

The front door opened and Shelby heard the sound of jackets being hung up on the hall stand. Her stomach tightened. "No, thank you. That's very kind but I think, since my cousin caused Bree's accident, I shouldn't be here longer than necessary."

Evie's mouth tightened for a moment. "What happened to Bree was a tragedy, for everyone, but God can make good out of it."

Shelby sighed. "That's what my mother would have said."

"You don't believe her?"

"She wanted to believe in the happy, God-will-provide kind of thing, but that didn't play out in our lives when my sister and I were younger. It took me a long time to understand." Even when they were eating canned beans for dinner. Even when their father left after the divorce and her mother had refused to let the girls go live with him, the woman had clung to her stubborn, rose-colored view of life.

Now that Shelby wasn't a child anymore, she had grown to respect her mother for believing God's promises. After all, Shelby and her sister grew up just fine. She wished desperately that she could tell her mother she'd been right, to ask forgiveness for dismissing her mother's staunch, faith-grounded optimism. Pain licked at her insides.

"She's, um, disabled now," Shelby said flatly. "She had a stroke that affected her brain. My sister was caring for her until we had to move her into a place with full-time nursing."

"Is your father still around?"

"He lives in Canada. I haven't seen him in a long time. I recently discovered that, uh, he isn't interested in being a father, never was."

"I'm sorry." Evie took her hand, the skin of her palms warm and calloused and comforting.

"Me, too, but my mother did her best trying to be Mom and Dad to us." Yet another thing she should have said before it was too late.

Evie hesitated and then took a breath. "You know, we have a lot of holiday fun around here. We host a Christmas Eve dinner for the town. I want to invite you to hang out with the Thorn clan. I mean, if you don't have plans with your uncle."

Shelby understood. Uncle Ken was not welcome here, for all Evie Thorn's assurances about God making it all turn out okay. Even the matriarch of the Thorn family blamed Uncle Ken for his son's actions.

So much for grace and forgiveness. Fine, the Arroyos didn't need grace, especially not from this family. She detached herself from Evie's grasp. "Thank you again. I'd better go and let you get lunch served."

She hustled to the front door, thinking she would escape before the brothers arrived in the kitchen for lunch. Barrett met her just as she stepped outside.

"Hello," he said politely.

She could not help but marvel at the electric blue of his eyes, the most brilliant hue, like the sky on the first day of summer vacation. His gaze seemed to pierce right through her. There was something in his look, something accusatory? Suspicious?

Distrustful, she decided. Fine. She did not trust him either, even though he had crawled into a ravine to haul her out. Her face went hot at the memory.

She held up her bundle. "Just picking up my clothes."

"You riding the Teke?"

"Yes. My uncle doesn't ride much anymore and Diamond needs it."

"Spirited horse, even if she is older."

She raised an eyebrow. "Are you implying I can't handle her?"

He shrugged. "Just observing. I remember hearing that your uncle bought her from Hatcher's wife a while back. Sold off a bunch of horses then."

"I didn't know who Uncle Ken bought her from, but I wonder why Hatcher or anybody would want to sell off a gorgeous horse like that."

"Wouldn't recommend asking him. You two haven't exactly hit it off."

She tossed her hair back. "He's going to be seeing more of me than he likes. I'm on my way to the police station later today. I'm going to ask Officer Larraby to come with me to force Hatcher to let me into that mine this afternoon."

"Oh."

"What?" She stared into the implacable blue gaze. "My uncle owns the mineral rights. Legally, Hatcher can't refuse me, and it's Larraby's job to uphold the law in this town, isn't it?"

No change of expression on his face. "Uh-huh."

"Would you care to elaborate on your 'uh-huh'?"

"Uh-uh."

She groaned. "You don't talk a whole lot, do you?"

"More than my brother Jack."

Now there was the tiny quirk to his mouth that indicated the hint of a smile.

Her annoyance ebbed. "Well, anyway, I'm going to do my job with or without Hatcher's consent." She reached for the door but he opened it first, ushering her outside.

"Even if it causes trouble?"

She shot him a look. "Would you stop caring for your horses if it meant trouble?"

"Never."

"Well, then, I guess we're on the same page." His face did not indicate as much. "Are you, I mean, is your back okay?"

"Only scratches."

She had the feeling Barrett would say that even if he'd nearly been cut in half. She untied Diamond and climbed into the saddle.

Barrett looked at her. His eyes were contemplative, tense. "Be careful. It's dangerous," he said.

"What's dangerous? Diamond or tangling with Hatcher?"

"Take your pick," he said.

"I can take care of myself," she said, wishing at once that she hadn't. Still, she did not see disdain or ridicule in his expression, only a glimmer of some emotion she could not name, buried deep.

Guiding Diamond home, pain throbbed in her temple and she tried not to think about the burning dynamite arcing toward her. Hatcher? Someone else? Who might be in the dense cover of trees watching her?

Waiting?

SIX

Barrett loaded two English saddles into the truck next to a case of homemade pickles and drove them to Hatcher's Saddlery to be oiled and tended before the next round of riding lessons started up after the holidays. The Gold Bar offered training in both Western-and English-style riding. With Christmas Eve just a week away, the chores were piling up. He'd promised to start working on putting up the tables for the holiday dinner. He'd not felt much holiday cheer at all since Bree died, but at least he was now able to enjoy his mother's pleasure at the festivities hosted on the ranch.

Joe Hatcher operated his saddlery out of a small building set on his sprawling acreage. A thick cluster of oak trees and shrubs screened the workshop from the residence where Hatcher lived with his daughter, Emmaline.

Barrett did not know Hatcher's ex-wife, Cora, well. Their families hadn't socialized much and Hatcher's divorce happened when Barrett was too steeped in Bree's death to pay much attention to such things. He had to believe it was hard to raise a kid alone, especially a girl who would grow into a woman just as hard to figure out as any other of her kind. *Women*, Barrett mused. *Who could possibly understand them?*

Barrett was surprised to see another truck already parked in front, a familiar fully loaded model with shiny green paint.

Ken Arroyo's vehicle.

Barrett debated whether or not to put his truck in Reverse and return another time. Instead he sucked in a breath as he heard loud voices coming from inside the saddlery. One was Joe Hatcher's low rumble and the other a higher-pitched, feminine timbre, which made his breath catch. Shelby? She had not waited for the police to accompany her before she confronted Hatcher with her plan. Barrett groaned inwardly. Typical.

Chris Larraby pulled up in his police vehicle next to Barrett. He hastened from the car and entered the shop. Barrett hesitated only a moment longer before he followed Larraby in.

"You need to be reasonable," Shelby was saying. She did a double take when she saw Barrett, but she did not move away from her position across the counter from Hatcher.

Hatcher looked anything but reasonable. His nostrils flared like an enraged bull's. "Don't care what your fancy papers say."

"That's why I asked Officer Larraby to come," Shelby said, calmly.

"Sorry I was late," Larraby said. "Something came up."

"Gonna strong-arm me, Chris?" Hatcher said.

"Nothing like that, Joe, just calm down."

Shelby shook her head. "I have a legal right to go in that mine and he's here to see that you comply."

"That right?" Hatcher said, staring at Larraby. "You gonna force me?"

"Let her do her thing," Larraby said. "She's within the law."

"And if you interfere," Shelby said, "you're breaking it." Her expression softened a bit. "Look, I don't want to make this hard on you. I'm here to assess the mine. That's all. That's my job."

Hatcher's eyebrows drew together in a scowl. "And if you decide there's gold worth mining down there, I have to let your uncle dig up my place?"

"That's not my decision to make. I'm only a fact finder."

"Well, find your facts somewhere else," he snapped. "I'm not gonna let you snoop around my property."

Shelby crossed her arms. "Why not, Mr. Hatcher? What are you so afraid that I will see?"

Time seemed to stop for a moment as the two locked eyes. Then Hatcher slammed a hand down on the counter. "I ain't afraid. It's the principle."

But Barrett had seen the evidence and he knew

Shelby had, too, the flash of emotion that darted across Joe Hatcher's face. Fear. What was the source, Barrett wondered.

He felt a presence at his elbow and looked down at the petite Emmaline. The blond-haired woman was probably in her early twenties, yet she had the appearance of a teen. She chewed her lip, arms folded protectively around her, brown eyes wide.

Barrett nodded at her. "A little disagreement. Going to be okay."

She gave him a grateful smile. "I hate yelling."

Probably heard a lot of that with Joe Hatcher for a father, Barrett figured.

Larraby's radio crackled and he listened to the dispatcher for a moment. "I have to go. Let the lady on your property."

"Now?" Hatcher demanded.

"Now."

"That an order?"

"I don't want to make it into one. Just do it."

Shelby and Barrett followed Larraby out to his car. Emmaline trailed behind.

"Thank you, Officer," Shelby said.

Larraby scowled. "Don't thank me. I don't like strangers coming into town and upsetting the locals. Personally, I would react the same way Joe is. Do what you need to do. Get in and get out."

Shelby's cheeks pinked, but she did not reply.

"Aren't you going to stay in case things go bad?" Barrett said.

"Joe's not going to do anything." Larraby yanked open his car door. "And I'm a cop, not a babysitter."

"This isn't safe, with everything that's happened," Barrett growled.

"If you're so concerned, you go with her." He slammed the door and drove away.

Hatcher stalked out of the saddlery. His face was splotched with anger.

"Are you taking me to the mine entrance now, Mr. Hatcher?" Shelby asked.

He didn't answer but his expression was murderous. He started up the gravel path that cut around the shop and into the trees. Rocks ground under his booted feet. He did not look back to see if Shelby was following.

"That's the way to the mine," Emmaline said, chewing her lip. "It's hard to find if you don't know what you're looking for."

Shelby smiled and thanked the young woman. "You must be Emmaline. They told me in town you lived here with your dad. I'm sorry I've caused so much ruckus."

"Daddy doesn't like ruckus unless he's the one causing it." She sighed. "Better catch up with him if you want to find the mine. I would go with you to help but…" She shivered. "My mom used to explore all the time. She was kind of an amateur geologist, I think. I never liked it. It's so lonely up there. There are strange sounds, and at night…" She shrugged.

"I'll make sure I'm not here at night," Shelby said

with a gentle smile at Emmaline. "Thank you. I'll go catch up with him." She hurried after Hatcher.

Barrett tried to think of something to say to stop her, but he came up blank.

Emmaline eyed the saddles in Barrett's truck. "Did you need those tended to, Mr. Thorn? If you bring them inside, I can write up your order."

"Thanks." Barrett hauled the saddles into the shop.

While Emmaline scrawled out the order on a notepad, he was thinking about Shelby.

It's so lonely up there.

In light of what had happened the previous night, Barrett was angry at Larraby for driving off and leaving Hatcher to lead the stubborn Shelby.

If you're so concerned, then you go with her.

He wasn't concerned, not about Shelby. The woman would do whatever she dreamed up, regardless. No, he wasn't worried about her.

Except that his stomach muscles were taut and the niggling in his nerves would not be ignored.

Barrett Thorn often thought he'd become another person since Bree died. An observer of life instead of a participator, a guy who let life roll past him like a river while he watched, rooted to the bank. But there was one thing that had not changed about him—that gut sense of right and wrong that his conscience would never let him ignore. Right now, his gut was hollering loud and clear that Shelby Arroyo should not be left in the hands of Joe Hatcher, no matter how much his father believed in Hatcher's character.

Sighing heavily, he thanked Emmaline and left the shop, grabbed a flashlight and his hat from his truck and headed up the slope the two had taken.

"Mr. Thorn," Emmaline called. "Are you going up there, too?"

"Yeah," he said, yanking his jacket zipper. "Looks like I am."

Shelby had to jog to catch up with Hatcher. She did not try to make small talk, just did her best not to slow his progress. As she trotted along, she could not help but wonder if the ground underneath her feet was laced with veins of quartz that might yield a rich gold strike, an assayer's dream. A tremor of excitement rippled through her at the thought that she might literally be standing above the answer to Uncle Ken's problems.

After several recent conversations, Uncle Ken had finally confided to her that his real estate business had been languishing. She knew the lawyers for Devon had been costly, too.

It stoked the feeling of guilt inside her. Uncle Ken had supplemented her meager earnings to pay for her college. He'd been more of a provider than her own folks, with her mother spending whatever money her father sent. She could never understand why her mother insisted that Shelby and Erin live with her instead of their father.

Why can't we just go live with Dad? she remembered shouting at her mother in one of her teenage fits. *He's got a steady job and he knows how to keep money in the bank. He misses us and you never even let us visit him.* It was bold talk since she'd only received a couple of letters and one phone call from her absent father.

Children belong with their mother, she would always reply. So when her mother frittered away yet another paycheck on new clothes for the girls or a trip to the zoo, Shelby would try to work even more hours at her part-time jobs.

It had not been enough to pay for school, so Uncle Ken stepped in. Erin had put off going to college because their mother's medical needs had been too great. When Shelby started to bring in an income that provided for her mother, she'd insisted her sister should delay her schooling no longer. Now it was Shelby's turn to funnel as much money as she could to both Erin and her mother. Shelby would help her make it through nursing school, after she got Uncle Ken's situation straightened out. Hopefully a rich vein of gold in the mine would recoup everything he'd invested in her.

Her throat thickened at the memory of his shrunken appearance when she'd arrived the week before. The toll of Devon's trial and imprisonment had cost Uncle Ken more than money. He was a shadow of the man he used to be.

Her thoughts were interrupted as she and Hatcher

crested a steep hill. Down below them was a scrub-covered gorge and in front, a crumbling stone cliff. Hatcher seemed to consider a moment before he plunged through the knee-high shrubs. Grateful that she had worn her hiking boots and a windbreaker, she fell in behind him.

As they walked farther into the untamed growth, she suppressed a shiver. Was she walking into the wilderness with the man who had attacked her, thrown dynamite at her? But the police knew the situation, so surely Hatcher would not risk his own freedom by harming her. Unless the man was just plain crazy, she thought uneasily.

They stopped at a spot where the ground and the cliff intersected. All she could see was a tangle of branches and wild grasses that came up to her thighs. Hatcher pushed aside the foliage.

"Here."

She peered beyond him. At the bottom of the cliff was a dark hole about six feet across and just about her height. Across the gap was an iron fence, screwed into the rock on each side, secured by a rusty padlock. Hatcher fished out a key ring from his pocket and selected a key. She thought his look turned calculating as he removed it from the ring and shouldered past her to unlock the padlock and wrench aside the fence.

"Well, now," he said with a smile. "In you go."

She hesitated, a blast of chilled air wafting out of the entrance. It was pitch-black inside. Her nerves screamed at her not to deliver herself into that gaping maw.

"I…"

"Whatsa matter?" He came closer. "You scared?"

"No. Are you coming, too?"

"Uh-uh. Wild animals in there," he said with a cunning smile. "Some of the tunnels are flooded, too. Real slippery-like. Old guy like me can't risk falling and breaking a hip, but you're young and strong and sure of yourself, ain't you?" He laughed a wet, crackling laugh. "Won't be a problem for you at all, going into the mine all alone."

"She's not going in alone."

Shelby whirled to see Barrett Thorn standing right behind Hatcher, his expression calm and implacable as always.

"You don't have to…" Shelby started. "I mean, I can go in by myself."

"Isn't right."

Barrett's lips drew together in a determined line. Shelby understood that there was no way she was going to change this cowboy's mind. She was not sure whether she should be flattered or infuriated. Somehow, the feeling that rose to the top was relief.

"Awww, ain't that chivalrous?" Hatcher said. "If you two are both stupid enough to want to crawl around that mine, then go right ahead. I'll be in the shop. If you need me, just whistle." He moved back, the grin still wide, allowing Shelby to step inside.

The darkness engulfed her immediately, so she

switched on her flashlight. Barrett crowded in behind, ducking to squeeze his head under the ceiling of stone.

Shelby beamed her flashlight above, the light sparking on the moisture seeping from the rock.

A loud clang shook the walls and made her cry out. They spun around to see Hatcher slam the gate and click the padlock closed.

SEVEN

Shelby was at the bars in a moment, striking her palm on the metal. Barrett crowded behind her.

"Open this gate," she yelled.

There was no answer, no sign of Hatcher.

"Hatcher," Barrett boomed, bracing his arms around her body and calling over her head. "You better unlock it right now before I kick it down." She could feel his breath warm on her neck, the anger turning his arms to steel.

Still no answer. Her heart hammered against her ribs. It was lunacy to lock them in here with the police knowing where they were. She'd left a note for Uncle Ken this time, as well. What was Hatcher trying to prove?

Barrett shouted again and to her relief, Hatcher appeared, laughing.

"No need to go all Rambo," he said, reaching for the padlock. "I was just joking around. You should have seen the look on your faces," he said. "I'll open it up."

He fiddled with the lock, bending closer until his nose was inches from the old metal. "Just one more minute… Oh." He stared at the lock and then straightened. "Would you look at that?" He held up the key, now broken in half. "Busted. Other half's stuck in the lock."

"And I'm supposed to believe that was an accident?" Shelby said.

"Don't matter what you believe, missy," he said. "Key's broken. Gonna have to go back to the workshop and get another. I think I got a spare somewhere in the back room. I'll just go get it, shall I?"

Shelby squashed the sensation of panic at being locked in. "Yes."

"And if you aren't back here in a half hour," Barrett snapped, "my brothers will come with a pair of bolt cutters if I don't have it kicked down myself."

"Sure, sure," Hatcher said, waving an airy hand. "Call 'em up on your cell, why don't you? I'll be back as quick as I can. You enjoy that mine now, Miss Arroyo." He left, whistling, his pace leisurely and relaxed.

Barrett kicked at the bars so hard Shelby almost screamed. Again and again he slammed his booted foot into the metal with such force it caused debris to rain down on them.

"Stop," she said, grabbing his arm. "It might be unstable."

He grunted in frustration.

Shelby got out her cell phone. "I have no signal here. You?"

Barrett stepped away, breathing hard, and checked his phone. "Nothing. That explains Hatcher's cat-in-the-cream look." Barrett's own look was that of a caged lion. "He knew we weren't going to be calling for help."

Shelby shook her head. "So we're really locked in here until he gets back?"

"Looks that way."

"And he's going to take his sweet time, isn't he?"

Barrett fisted his hands on his hips, flashing her a look of pure exasperation. "Well, what did you expect?"

"I didn't expect a welcome mat, but I figured with the cops here, he would comply at least."

Barrett's eyes blazed in the gloom. "You forced his hand. That wasn't smart. He threatened to kill you, and here you were ready to climb inside an abandoned mine all by yourself."

Tipping her head up so she could look him in the eye, she folded her arms across her chest. "You don't have to yell. I didn't ask you to come."

She heard his teeth grind together. "I'm not yelling. I'm talking forcefully."

"Well, you can stay here and talk forcefully to yourself. I'm going to look around."

He caught her hand. "Not a good idea."

Her pulse skittered as she felt the strength in his grip, caught the musky scent of his soap. "You don't get to give me commands. I'm not one of your horses."

"Horses would have more sense."

She pulled away. "This is what I came here to do, locked in or not. I might as well make use of the time." She turned before he could toss back an answer. He was right, of course, she had forced Hatcher into a corner, but there hadn't seemed to be another choice. His reluctance to let her in surpassed mere orneriness. The guy was desperate to hide something.

Her flashlight picked out a downward slanting tunnel that disappeared to the left. It was high enough for her to walk easily, the stone walls glimmering with moisture. The air was chilled and damp, but she sucked in a deep breath of it anyway. It was the fragrance of things long hidden and undisturbed. For some reason she found it comforting, always had.

"Owww," Barrett said, and she realized he was a few steps behind her.

"Ceiling's a little low here."

"Thanks," he said, taking off his hat and rubbing a hand across his forehead.

"I really don't need an escort," she said stiffly. *Especially not a disgruntled cowboy.*

"Oh, I think you do."

"I'm not helpless."

"More like disaster prone."

She did not dignify that with an answer. There

might be a whiff of truth to it anyway, since she'd been in a perpetual mess since she came to Gold Bar.

Barrett ducked around a low-hanging cone of rock. "What are you looking for?"

"Oh, you know, big chunks of gold sticking out of the walls. Jewels, maybe, like that scene from Snow White."

"I'm not an idiot," he snapped. "I know a little about the mining process."

She could not resist a smile. "Sorry. Just trying to lighten the mood. I'm getting acclimated right now. Looking at the formations, the layering in the rock. I'll probably drill for a sample later, but right now a hand grab would work."

"All right. Grab the nearest rock and let's get back to the entrance."

"Why the rush? Scared, cowboy?" she said, raising an eyebrow, enjoying teasing him.

"Not scared, smart. The rock is sopping wet and slippery, or didn't you notice?"

"I did," she said. "I'm hoping the lower levels of the mine aren't completely flooded."

"Then let's be smart about it and come back tomorrow with battery-powered flashlights, rubber-soled shoes and someone standing guard at the fence."

"Right now I want to see what's around the corner."

He stopped as if he'd got an electric shock.

"What?" His face was stark in the glow of her flashlight. "What's wrong?"

"Nothing."

She touched him on the shoulder to keep him from turning away. "Not nothing."

He rubbed a hand over his close-cropped beard. "I, uh, my late wife, Bree. She was always saying that the best was right around the corner." The dripping water marked the seconds of silence.

"I'm sorry," Shelby said. "I didn't mean to cause you pain."

He looked away. "Not pain, so much. Less now anyway. More like..." He shook his head. "I'm not so good with words."

She wanted to touch a hand to his chest, to let him know that she understood. "It's hard to find the words when your life gets flipped upside down."

He cocked his head. "You, too?"

She didn't want to tell him about her father. How could the impact of what she'd learned about him possibly be on par with the loss of a spouse? Choosing her words with precision, she tried to explain. "I believed something that was a lie for a long time and I blamed my mother, misjudged her and now... it's too late. I can't fix it. It's just too late." She was horrified to feel tears pricking her eyelids.

"Hey," he said, taking her free hand. In spite of the cold air, his fingers were warm on hers.

"I'm a black-and-white kind of person," she babbled. "And I was sure, so sure, my mother was selfishly keeping us from our father, but now that she's impaired, well, I learned…" She swallowed hard. "Never mind. Family drama. Too messy to talk about. Let's just say I have regrets."

"I get that. After Bree died, I got mired down in that feeling. All the things I could have done, should have done." He cupped her hand in his hard, calloused palm. "If I've learned one thing it's that we can't live in regret. God doesn't want that for our lives."

She wanted to let those words loose inside and allow them to find the hurt place that throbbed bright with pain. Instead something completely different came out of her mouth. "I am sure my cousin Devon regrets what he did," she said quietly.

The distance sprang up between them, as thick and solid as the stone walls. She knew she should not have brought it up, but her comment lay between them like a ticking time bomb. He let go of her hand and stared at the slick stone under his feet.

Barrett finally spoke. "I do believe that Devon is sorry. He wrote me a couple of letters from prison. Took me a long time to be able to read them. I've really been praying that I can fully forgive him someday. I'm on my way, I think."

She wondered if she would be strong enough to forgive such a thing. Not on her own, she was certain. "Uncle Ken says the accident destroyed Devon, too. He'd give anything to undo what he did."

Barrett stared at her. "What about your uncle?"

"I don't know what you mean."

Barrett's voice grew hard as stone. "Does he regret his part in my wife's death?"

"His part?"

The whites of his eyes glinted like hard marble. "Your uncle coddled Devon. Bought him anything. Horses, cars. Never set limits. Made him think he never had to pay the price for his misbehavior."

"You don't know that."

"Yes, I do," he said bitterly. "Good old Daddy paid for Devon's speeding tickets, fixed his car when he banged it up, let him live at home with no job, no purpose but having fun."

She recoiled at the acid in his tone. "That's not true."

"It is. Your uncle didn't do his job as a parent and it cost me everything. Never once has he expressed regret for enabling his son to kill my wife."

The quiet was broken only by the sound of trickling water and the low moan of a draft wafting through the tunnels. She was chilled down deep to the bone.

"Maybe you're right about exploring today," she said softly. "We should wait by the entrance for Hatcher to come back. I'll just look around the corner. You go ahead back and I'll catch up."

She hastily moved a pace up the trail, not wanting Barrett to see the emotions she battled.

Uncle Ken had been a permissive father, she knew. His wife died of a hemorrhage giving birth to Devon and he'd tried to make it up to the boy in every way he could. Maybe it was a family trait.

That thought startled her. Was that what her own mother had tried to do? Shower her girls with nice things to fill the hole left by their father's departure? *No, not departure, abandonment*, she corrected. The pain pinched her heart again.

That was a different situation, she told herself angrily. Devon was a good kid, kind and generous like his father, charming and funny to boot. Barrett was wrong about Uncle Ken. He'd tried his best like any parent. She would not bring up the topic again and she would make sure Barrett was not her escort when she returned for more samples.

Her next footstep landed on a narrow strip of rock and the one after that, on nothing at all.

Barrett heard Shelby's sharp intake of air and he was moving as she started to fall. His fingers grazed her shoulder, her sleeve, and he scrambled for a handhold, finally grasping the hem of her jacket. Too late. She catapulted into the darkness below. Because he would not allow himself to let go, he tumbled through the gap in her wake.

The fall was maybe fifteen feet, ending with a frigid splash into neck-deep water. His boot heels hit the bottom with a jarring thud. Shelby popped up next to him, heaving in a breath, coughing and choking.

He grabbed her elbow to keep her from ducking under the surface again. The water leveled off just under his chin, which meant it would be up to the crown of her head. He pulled her close. "Hold around my neck."

She did, still coughing.

"Hurt?"

"No," she gasped. "Cold."

"Yeah." The water had to be somewhere in the neighborhood of forty degrees and she was already shivering violently. His skin prickled. They did not have much time before their body temperatures would drop dangerously low. "Got your phone? I lost mine."

"Yes," she said, teeth chattering. She pulled it out from her back pocket and touched a button. "It's wet, but still working." A tiny glow punched through the gloom. "Unfortunately, we don't have coverage down here."

"At least the flashlight works," Barrett said, but the dot of light did not have much impact.

The dark was so profound that he could not see more than the vague white gleam of her face right next to his. He clamped his right arm around her waist and pulled his left up above the water line.

"Can you push the button on my watch?"

She did and the illuminated face let off a scant glow. It was enough for him to see that they were in a lower tunnel with smooth walls. About six feet past them, a ladder leading up into the darkness was bolted to the wall. "Keep pushing the button if you can."

She did, though her hands were trembling. "And here I thought watches were obsolete."

"Some people say the same about cowboys."

She managed a giggle and it made him feel better somehow.

He sloshed closer to the ladder, holding her with one arm, his elbow bumping something. She lost her grip on his watch light as he moved to snatch at it. "Flashlight," he said triumphantly. He flicked it to life, catching her surprised smile.

"It still works?" she said.

"It was my granddaddy's flashlight. Tough as he was."

"Are all the Thorn men so tough?"

"Yep, but not as tough as the women."

Another giggle, this time softer. She was weakening from the cold.

He shined the light upward. The ladder led to an upper tunnel that vanished into the darkness. The rungs looked to be sturdy enough, though they had to be rusted in the face of all this moisture. He pushed on one with his foot and it held against the pressure.

"Here's the flashlight. Climb up slowly," he told her. "One rung at a time. It may not hold all the way to the top, but at least it will get you out of the water." He helped her settle her feet onto the lower slats. Climbing gingerly, one step up at a time, she advanced almost to the top.

"It connects to another tunnel," she called down. "I can't see much, but the air feels warmer so maybe it leads out."

"Climb in if you think it's safe."

She continued on to the top. Once there, she lay on her belly, shining the light down for him. "Your turn."

He climbed up, the metal groaning under his weight. The cold made his legs feel like they were made of stone. He pushed on, boots slipping against the iron.

With a loud shriek, the rung under his right foot gave way and he tumbled back into the water with a splash. He heard Shelby scream above him. He wanted to reassure her, but the cold and the impact took the breath clean out of him.

She was halfway down the ladder before he managed to stand, coughing and spluttering. "Stop. Don't come any farther, the ladder's not in good shape."

She froze. "Are you okay?"

"I've been better, but nothing broken I think. Go back up. I'm right behind you."

She ascended again and he picked his steps carefully, skipping over the busted slat and getting to the top without any further incident. He heaved himself up to join her on the ledge. His wet clothes clung to him, his boots waterlogged and soggy. He huffed out a breath as he considered. "This is terrible."

"I know." She groaned. "I have no idea which way is out."

"Not that. I lost my hat."

To his surprise, she started to giggle.

"That funny?"

"Well, you could have been killed falling off the ladder and right now we may be closing in on hypothermia, but you're most upset about your hat."

"It's my favorite hat," he said to clarify. "I got it all broken in just right."

She laughed afresh, the sound light and airy in the dank atmosphere of the mine. He cracked a smile as he looked around, but he couldn't find too much amusement in it. Her comment about hypothermia wasn't too far off.

He recalled the time when he was just a teen and Gold Bar experienced torrential rain for days. His family had helped the woefully overworked volunteer fire department rescue a man from where he'd been trapped in a waterlogged storage room. The man had died from hypothermia.

"I don't mean to ruin your happy mood, but we need to figure out a way out of here," he said. "Any ideas?"

They both looked as far as they could see in both directions. The tunnel stretched away into the darkness but by now he hadn't got a clue as to which avenue, if either, led back to the surface.

Shelby did not look as though she had a clue either.

"I was hoping you would have a plan," she said through chattering teeth.

A disoriented assayer and a clueless cowboy. It was turning into a mighty long afternoon.

EIGHT

Shelby did not think she'd ever been so cold in all her life. Her hands and feet were numb and even her breath felt cool when she blew into her hands. She wanted to curl up in a ball on the ground, but Barrett would not let her. He pulled her close and chafed her shoulders, rubbing his cheek against hers. "Gotta keep moving."

"Your beard tickles."

"Don't complain. It's warming you up, isn't it?"

"I'm not sure which way is out," she said, allowing her head to drop down against his chest. "I'm… I'm sorry for getting you into another jam."

His arms were strong around her body as he cradled her close, tucking her head under his chin. "Doesn't matter much, 'cept you owe me a hat."

"If we manage to get out of here, I'll buy you a new one, I promise."

"Deal." He stepped away, unzipped his jacket and put it around her shoulders. "It's still wet, but maybe another layer will help."

"No, I can't take it," she said, eyeing the soggy flannel of his shirt. "You'll freeze."

"Too stubborn to freeze. Just ask my mom." He zipped her firmly up to the chin and slid on the hood for good measure. "There. You could be in a fashion show."

She fingered the buttons on his shirtfront. "You must really like this clothing company. It's the same style you were wearing when you pulled me out of the ravine."

He ducked his head and examined the shirt as if he'd forgotten what he was wearing. "Got ten shirts all the same 'cept the color."

"Really?" Shelby goggled. "You like it that much?"

"Can't stand to shop. When my mom drags me into a store and I find one that fits, I get a lot of them."

She started to laugh but her body was too cold to cooperate.

"We've got to get out of here somehow," she muttered. With great effort, she forced her limbs into action, running her numb fingers over the stone walls, straining to get some glimmer from either direction that would help them determine an exit. The fall had disoriented her and she simply could not get her bearings. Barrett played the light over the black stone surface. It caught on a flash of color.

"Wait," she said. "What's that?"

He trained the light again, stopping on a small red

mark, a splotch the size of a dime. "That couldn't have been here from the mining days, it's too fresh."

She pointed. "And there's another one."

Barrett followed her along, playing the light over the walls.

She peered closely at the colored spots. "There's another one, ten feet away. What do you think they're for?"

"Dunno. I don't see any in the other direction."

"They're not like any official markings I've ever seen. Maybe some kids got down here? Should we follow?"

"That's your call. I'd say we don't go more than fifty yards past the ladder. Don't want to get even more lost," he said.

"There's either lost or found. No such thing as more lost or less lost."

He shook his head. "You don't spend much time in the woods, do you?"

She was about to retort when Barrett grabbed her arm. "Did you hear that?"

"What?"

"Listen."

They both strained to hear.

"Mr. Thorn." The voice floated like a wisp of fog through the tunnel. It was high-pitched, breathy. It made the skin on the back of her neck prickle.

"Who's there?" Barrett called out.

"This way," the voice called again. It was followed by a sound, a soft thud, like someone whacking a rock against another.

At first Shelby could not tell where the sound originated. She placed her palms on the rocks in different places until she was rewarded by a faint vibration.

"Over there," Shelby said, hardly able to contain her excitement. "It's coming from up the passage."

He went first, following the tunnel away from the ladder, beaming the flashlight at the rock projections so he didn't brain himself again. Shelby followed, her fingers holding on to his belt. Her legs were rubbery and weak but she tried to keep up the pace as best she could.

They stopped when they lost the tapping sound.

"I don't hear it anymore," he said. "Do you?"

"No, but the air here is warmer and I think the slope is heading up toward the surface."

Another tap, this time with a voice following. "Hurry. You've got to hurry."

They pushed as fast as they could, stumbling now and then on the dark rock, easing around occasional puddles and broken bits of wood.

When Shelby saw the first glimmer of light, she almost cheered. As they hurried along, the view changed from pitch-black to light gray. They looked above their heads and saw a half-moon-shaped cutout in the rock wall about six feet above them, a threshold between the mine and the glorious surface. It had never before occurred to her that the sunshine was utterly magnificent.

A memory shot through her brain, a little prayer her mother had taught her about thanking God for the golden sun. She'd forgotten to be thankful lately, allowing too many other things to get in the way. When they got directly underneath the opening, Barrett cupped his hands. "Come on. I'll boost you."

"But how will you get out?"

"You'll go get my brothers or call the cops."

"But you could be hypothermic by then."

"I'll try to avoid that."

"But…"

He put a finger to her lips. "Ma'am, this is the way it's gonna be. You're climbing out right now, or I'm going to have to try to shove you through that hole and that's gonna be awkward for both of us."

She closed her mouth. Her determination was nothing compared to his ruthless cowboy chivalry. He would not go until she did. Period.

Before he could protest, she unzipped his jacket and handed it to him. "In case the rescue takes a while. You promise you're not going to die, right?"

"I will do my best, ma'am."

Acting under some impulse she did not understand, she brushed a kiss across his lips.

He didn't say anything, but she felt the echoes of a tender yearning in him, or was it in herself?

"Come on now," he said, voice low and throaty. "Quit stalling. Time for you to get out of here."

* * *

Ignoring the lingering tingle on his lips from her kiss, Barrett cupped his hands again and she stepped into them. He lifted her easily and after some wriggling, she made it out. Relief flooded through him. He could hear hollering now, and at first he was worried that Hatcher might be up there until Keegan's face appeared above him in the opening, silhouetted in brilliant sunlight.

"And I thought we were in the ranching business. Decided to try your hand at gold mining, Barrett? You want a little pickax for Christmas?"

Barrett's teeth were chattering too hard for him to rustle up much of an answer. Keegan lowered a rope and in a matter of moments he was hoisted out into the daylight, which nearly blinded him.

His father threw a blanket around him. Shelby was already swaddled in a second blanket, he was happy to see. She appeared alert and interested, all good signs. In fact, her relief at the sight of him was written across her face clear as the words on a page.

Barrett filed that thought away for later and tried to stop shivering. "How'd you f-f-find us?"

Keegan jutted his chin. "You can thank her. She called us and then led us to you."

Emmaline moved closer. "Daddy came back for the key. He wasn't, um, in a big hurry, so I sneaked away and called Mr. Thorn. Then I ran back to the main entrance but you two weren't there. I knew about this other way to get in. I used to explore when I was braver." Her smile was shaky.

"Thank you, Emmaline," he said. "I think you were pretty brave, especially since your dad might be mad at you for helping us."

"Never mind," she said, an unexpected spark of determination in her eyes. "I did what I had to do."

"And Shelby and I appreciate it," he said.

Shelby nodded over chattering teeth. "We sure do. Thank you, Emmaline."

Hatcher ambled over with Officer Larraby at his side.

Larraby eyed them. "Came to check on you. Hatcher said he lost the spare key. What happened?"

"They almost got killed is what happened," Keegan snapped. "Could have kept an eye on Hatcher to make sure this didn't happen, couldn't you?" The anger in his tone brought an answering glare from Larraby.

"Not my job to tend to your family, Keegan." Larraby put a slight stress on the word *your*.

The two were biological half brothers, though Larraby's father had never publicly acknowledged Keegan as his child. The rage that simmered between them marked them as enemies.

The last thing they needed at the moment was more antagonism. Barrett hastened to intervene. "This is Hatcher's responsibility, not Larraby's."

Hatcher rolled his eyes. "The key broke. I was looking for the spare. It was an accident, like I said.

You two were fool enough to go up against the mine and the mine won. Your fault, so don't blame it on me."

"You're not an innocent party here, Hatcher," Keegan started. His father put a calming hand on his arm, but it was Shelby who spoke.

"He's right. I shouldn't have gone wandering without being prepared. Barrett said the same thing, but he came along reluctantly to make sure I was okay. This isn't Mr. Hatcher's fault, at least, not all of it."

Barrett gaped at her.

Hatcher nodded. "Now that you've seen how dangerous the mine is, I guess you're done with this fool business?"

"For now," Shelby said.

Barrett didn't buy it for a second. Those captivating green eyes shone with a determination that said Hatcher might have won the skirmish but she would never let him win the war. He had to admire her spark, as much as he did not want to admit it.

"Good," Larraby said. "I've got other things to do than come out here on a regular basis. Do either of you need medical attention?"

Both Barrett and Shelby refused to go to the clinic, so Larraby departed. Barrett insisted on driving Shelby back to her uncle's place himself.

"Just to make sure you're done wreaking havoc for today," he told her. Owen followed in Ken's pickup, though the look on his face said he wasn't happy about it.

It jolted Barrett to think how Bree's death had affected all of them, carving a line of hatred between the Thorns and the Arroyos that rippled across both families. How was it that he could begin to pray for forgiveness for Devon, but refuse to do so for Ken?

Because Ken doesn't deserve it, he told himself fiercely.

He opened the passenger door for Shelby.

"What are the pickles for?" she said as she slid in, eyeing the case in the back.

"Oh, uh, I'm bringing them to the church. They run a soup kitchen and, er, we have a lot of pickles."

"Homemade, huh? Your mom?"

"Well, actually, no. I made them." He waited for the reaction he knew was coming.

"You make pickles? I'm impressed. How did you learn to do that?"

He sighed. "After Bree died, I sort of withdrew from life. The only thing I wanted to think about was the horses. I guess I got to worrying everyone because they did this intervention type thing and demanded I either join a line dancing group or pick a hobby."

"You're not up for line dancing."

"I'd rather be boiled in oil. I found an old cookbook of my grandma's and the first ten pages were all pickles, so I figured I'd give it a try."

"That's incredible."

"Yeah. I made so many pickles it filled the entire pantry. We gave them away to everyone we could until people started hiding when they saw me coming. It's, uh, kind of a family joke now."

"Perfect. I really needed a chuckle."

He blasted the heater and Shelby pressed her fingers right up to the vent. Her eyes closed in pleasure. "I will never take warmth for granted again. Thank You, God," she breathed.

Yes, he thought, *thank You*.

Enough of the light and easy conversation. "So what are you plotting?" he said.

"What do you mean?" Her face was as innocent as a newborn lamb's.

"You know good and well what I mean. You gave up too easily with Hatcher. What scheme are you cooking up?"

"I'm scheming to take a hot bath, for one, complete with bubbles and a rubber ducky if I can find one."

"No jokes. Spill it."

"Barrett Thorn," she said, "just because you're too stubborn to freeze does not mean I owe you anything."

"Oh, yes, you do."

"What?"

"I lost my favorite hat because of you."

Her face lit with a gorgeous smile that did something to his insides.

"You got me there. Okay, so I owe you a hat, but not an explanation."

They pulled up in the gravel drive, Owen right behind. Diamond grazed along the fence, cropping grass with an elegance characteristic of her breed. Lovely, hot-blooded, strong and intelligent. Like Shelby, he thought unexpectedly. He blinked hard and fiddled with the steering wheel.

She hopped out of the truck before he could get out to open the passenger door for her. Leaning in, she gave him a rueful smile.

"Thank you, Barrett. It seems like I'm always thanking you."

"I'll try not to let it go to my head."

She laughed. "You go on with your pickle deliveries, cowboy. Don't worry about me."

"But, Shelby," he said before she got away, "joking aside, you aren't planning on going back in that mine, are you?"

Her smile vanished. Up went her chin. "I am going to keep my promise to my uncle."

"Even if it kills you?"

Shutting the door, she walked purposefully toward the house without looking back.

NINE

Shelby was grateful that Uncle Ken was closed in his office when she let herself into the house. If he knew what had transpired in the mine, he would have forbidden her to return. Tiptoeing upstairs to the guest room, she sank into the hottest bath possible and stayed there until her toes turned to prunes. Dressed in clean clothes with her hair washed and dried, she returned to find Uncle Ken in the dining room with a small duffel bag.

"Hello, Shelby," he said, sinking into an armchair. "I didn't hear you come in. I was just paying some bills." He offered a wry smile. "Could use a gold mine right about now."

"I'm going to make that happen if I can, Uncle Ken."

"I know you will."

She pointed to the bag. "Going on a trip?"

"I have to fly to England. I have property there that's up for sale and I'm signing papers. I really don't feel right about leaving you now, but I have to make this deal happen." His smile was sheepish. "I've got some creditors that won't be put off anymore. I'll be back in five days, tops."

"It's okay. I'll be perfectly fine."

"All right. Zeke will be by tomorrow morning to check on the horses. He'll come morning and evening to tend to them and get them settled for the night. Diamond is a handful so I don't want you trying to deal with her all by yourself."

"Did you buy Diamond from Joe Hatcher, Uncle Ken?"

"From his ex-wife, Cora. Her father died and left her a dozen horses, all beautiful. Couldn't believe she wanted to sell and I didn't really need any more, but Diamond was too beautiful to resist. Her daughter, Emmaline, was sure attached to that horse. Never made sense to me, but I'm not a man who can pass up a specimen like that. She's spirited, though, so be careful when you ride her."

"I've already reintroduced myself to Diamond. We get along fine."

The clock over the mantel bonged. She thought how dark and dreary the room looked without the barest hint of any holiday decorations.

"Well, I'd better go. Are you sure you'll be okay here?"

"I'll be fine. I want to do some research on the area geology anyway."

"So nothing dangerous up your sleeve, right?"

She wriggled her fingers. "Nope. Nothing dangerous."

He sighed, the late-afternoon sunlight catching the careworn creases in his face. There was no harder job than being a parent, she thought. It made her long for her mother.

"Uncle Ken," she said suddenly. "Did you know my father well?"

He arched an eyebrow. "Eric? No, not really." He drummed nervously on the table.

"My sister found—" she forced down a lump in her throat "—letters from my father. All this time I thought my mother was preventing us from living with Dad because she was selfish and didn't want to be alone."

"But the letters proved otherwise, didn't they?" Ken said softly.

"Yes. Did you know?" She caught his gaze, her own eyes wet.

"Your mother didn't out-and-out say so, but I suspected."

"He didn't want us. He said as much in the letters. He stopped sending money and left us to my mother, who made it sound like it was her decision to keep us from Dad. She lied because... To shelter us from knowing that our father didn't want us." Shelby had not said it aloud to anyone but her sister, Erin. The words stung like a scorpion.

Didn't want us.

Unwanted. The most painful word in the English

language. What hurt more was knowing how she'd fought her mother tooth and nail, blaming her for being selfish when the truth was the exact opposite. But her mother shouldn't have lied, should she? Would the truth have changed anything? Would Shelby have believed it?

Her uncle was shaking his head. "I can't imagine not wanting a child. Opal and I, we tried for years to have a baby. Opal lost five to miscarriages and it devastated both of us every time. People say they aren't really babies when they aren't fully formed, but that's not true. Each heartbeat was our child's and we grieved when none of the babies survived."

She sat next to him and took his hand. He looked at her through tears. "And then there was Devon. He represented the best day of my life, and the worst. I had what I'd prayed so hard for, and I lost my wife at the same time."

"I'm sorry."

"I tried every day to show him that I loved him. I guess I didn't do some things right, but I wasn't supposed to go it alone, you see?" His tone was pleading. "Opal was supposed to be my partner in it."

She clenched his fingers.

"And now..." He waved a hand around. "Well, he's got another year in prison but what will his life be like after? He can't even hold his head up after what happened."

"He'll learn to forgive himself," she murmured. Forgiveness, there was that word again, though she did not feel she had the right to use it. "And maybe some good will come out of it somehow."

Ken stared at her, hollow eyed. "'And we know that all things work together for good to those that love God, to those who are called according to His purpose.' Romans 8:28," he recited. "Do you believe that?"

She did not know how to answer. Her past and present and all the things that had happened at the Gold Bar seemed to have jumbled up her thoughts. "I'm not sure, but I want to."

"Opal said the good comes from becoming more like Jesus." He pressed her hand to his forehead. "I don't see Devon becoming anything. He's broken, he's ruined."

"But he's asked Barrett for forgiveness. That's a first step."

Ken wrenched away. "I know Barrett will never forgive him."

"I think he will, Uncle Ken. He's already started the process."

Ken's face was clouded in disbelief. "No, he won't. And Barrett blames me, too."

She stayed silent.

"Well, I am not guilty of anything but loving my son," Ken said, getting to his feet, "and I will never seek forgiveness for that. Not from God and not from Barrett Thorn."

He grabbed his bag and stalked to the door. With

his hand on the knob he turned back, eyes like slabs of granite, sparkling with rage.

"Don't let the Thorn family fool you, Shelby. They hate me, they hate Devon, and for all their religious spouting, that will never change."

The door slammed behind him.

The horses watched Barrett with their usual complacent curiosity on Saturday morning as he stacked the bales of hay in the feed room, checking for leaks in the roof. He always had a sense of peace when he worked on or near the horses, a feeling that everything was right as it should be, the universe in perfect order.

Friday had passed quietly, the routine chores of the ranch helping him forget his and Shelby's near-fatal experience in the mine. Now as the weekend before Christmas dawned in a swirl of pink and gold, he was not completely at ease. Though he'd heard nothing from Shelby since their escape from the mine on Thursday, he knew she was cooking up a plan and he also knew deep down in his gut that Joe Hatcher would do anything to get in her way.

What was driving the man? The question circled in his brain. Pride? Paranoia? Stubbornness? Heaving the bales of hay worked his muscles, but it did not seem to clarify his thinking. Finishing the loading job, he saw his father preparing the trailer, so he joined him.

"Taxi job?"

His father nodded. "Returning Brownie. She's ready to go home."

Barrett fetched the mare and led her to the trailer. Brownie was a beloved horse on the Bar Seven Ranch, a nice piece of property owned by a married couple who ran a dental practice. Doctors Joan and Bobby Kinley traveled when they could and Brownie was a regular customer because he required daily medication and specialized care that their other horses did not. The bay had been fearful of the trailer at first, but after hours of patient work by Barrett and Jack, Brownie was a self-loader, though Barrett still kept a wary eye.

Walking next to the horse, he offered encouragement and gentle pressure on the animal's flank until Brownie walked into the trailer. "That's a girl, Brownie," he praised, giving her a scratch as he secured the lead rope and closed the tailgate.

"Can you stand some company, Dad?"

His father chuckled. "Sure, unless you're going to pressure me like Keegan does about allowing four-wheeling on the property."

"No, sir. I'll take four hooves over four wheels any day."

Barrett climbed into the passenger seat and they rumbled slowly away from the ranch.

"Can I ask you a question, Dad?"

"Fire away."

"What do you know about Joe Hatcher?"

His father shifted a little in the seat. "I don't know

as it's right for me to talk about someone else's life, son. Don't know as I'd want someone to hash out mine when I wasn't there to defend myself."

"Not gossip, just facts. How's that?"

"All right. The facts." His father's calloused hands played with the steering wheel. "Joe lived on his dad's property, inherited the land and the saddlery business. Met his gal, Cora—" he squinted in thought "—Cora Felton, when her father came to the area looking for a place to stable his horses. Joe was in his late thirties when they married, I think, and Cora somewhat younger. Your mother would know the details."

"Okay. So they settled on Joe's place?"

"Yeah. Cora's dad died when Emmaline was real little and Cora inherited his horses."

"Were they, uh, happily married?"

"Not for me to say. Cora kind of kept to herself. Used to travel often, I know." He eased the truck and trailer toward the main part of town. "Joe stayed back with Emmaline and the horses when she would travel. When Emmaline graduated high school, Cora up and sold the horses, every last one of them."

"Why?"

"Dunno. Practical decision maybe. Horses aren't an inexpensive hobby, as you well know."

He knew, but that would not stop him from going without food or water before he walked away from his horses. Bree had felt the same, though she hadn't grown up with horses and she was always a little fearful around them except for Swanny.

His father continued, "After the horses were sold, she left town for good. That was almost five years ago. Haven't seen her since. Heard they divorced, but Joe doesn't talk about it. He's a proud man."

"Can you think of a reason why he's so reluctant to allow Shelby to survey the mine?"

His father raised an eyebrow. "Would you want a stranger coming onto the Gold Bar who could potentially give the green light to a mining operation?"

He considered. "No, sir, but if the law says she has the right, I wouldn't stand in her way."

"Joe will come around. He just needs to blow off steam about it so he feels like a man. Rough having your wife divorce you." He sighed. "If your mom left me alone to raise the four of you, I'd probably go a little berserk, too."

Barrett chuckled. "Yeah, we've been more than a handful, haven't we?"

"That's an understatement." His dad ran a hand over the crown of his head. "All this white hair came directly from the Thorn sons' shenanigans." He laughed. "But you're all God-fearing, honorable men who know right from wrong, so I guess we've done okay."

"Yes, sir, you have."

His father was never effusive, but Barrett could hear the pride in his dad's voice. Tom Thorn was a tough man, quietly passionate about God, his family and major-league baseball. He would, and had, dropped boxes of food anonymously on people's doorsteps if he heard they were hungry and stepped in to raise an unwanted child when the Thorns were struggling to keep the Gold Bar afloat. Barrett's parents had always been and always would be his heroes.

They were traveling through the sleepy main street, past the ancient oak tree outlined with colored lights when Barrett saw Ella Cahill entering the Sunrise Cafe coffee shop. "Dad, would you mind letting me out here? I'll catch up with you in a bit."

"All right."

Barrett got out, noticing his father eyeing the window of the Treasure Trove Gift Store.

"Uh, Dad?"

"Yes?"

"Mama said to tell you that she doesn't want any more aprons or scented candles for Christmas."

His father's mouth quirked. "Oh, yes? And what does your mama want for Christmas then, Barrett? I'm sure she gave you explicit marching orders."

What did his mother really want? For her sons to be married, he thought. For the house to be filled with grandchildren, for a daughter-in-law she could love as much as she had adored Bree. He swallowed. "She said she'd settle for a new checkerboard since the other got water damaged up in the attic."

His father laughed and then grew thoughtful. "So she's hankering for another family game night?"

They hadn't had one since Bree was killed. For a moment, Barrett was transported back in time, hearing the click of checkers, the crackling of the fire, Frank Sinatra singing holiday carols and the laughter of a family celebrating Christmas together. His mother was ready to resurrect some of that joy, to put the pain in its proper place.

Was he ready? Part of him thought so. The grief would never go away but now it was not the core of his being. There was something else burning deep inside, though. Anger at Ken still flamed in his heart, forgiveness he could not offer. He was not ready and was not sure he ever would be.

God help me, his soul whispered.

His father looked at him as though he knew exactly what Barrett was thinking, the acid feelings about Ken. "All right," he said softly. "I guess it's time. Your mama will get her new checkerboard." He hesitated. "You okay, son?"

"Yes, sir," Barrett said, even though his heart was very far from agreeing.

TEN

Barrett caught up with Ella as she finished ordering her frappe-latte-whatever-it-was and counting out her payment in coins. Aside from water, he'd only ever understood the values of coffee, black and as strong as he could get it, and ice-cold root beer on a sizzling summer day. The barista handed her the steaming beverage.

She gazed at the drink with a look of rapture and he realized this was a treat for her. He wished he'd got there a moment earlier to purchase it for her. Money was tight for Ella and it had been ever since she'd been a kid. Nothing came easy for her or her sister, never had.

"Ella. Got a minute?"

She carefully snapped a plastic lid on her cardboard cup. "Sure, Barrett. Everything okay with the horses?"

"Yeah, this is about another thing."

"Yeah?" A mischievous smile crossed her face. "Are you wanting some help tuning up your truck?"

"No, thank you. I still have the notes you gave me from last time." When it came to engines, Ella was as good as or better than him or any of his brothers, and that was saying something.

"I, uh, I wondered what Shelby Arroyo was giving you the third degree about yesterday."

She tucked a strand of red hair behind her ear. "Maybe I shouldn't have mentioned it. She wasn't rude or anything. It just surprised me since, I mean, your family isn't exactly tight with the Arroyos."

"It's okay. I was just wondering."

"She wanted to know if we had a history museum of some kind, where old documents are kept."

"Documents?"

"Like topographical maps."

His stomach contracted. "Oh."

"So I told her to go talk to Shep. He'd be the guy to have them, wouldn't he?"

"Yeah, I suppose so. Thanks, Ella."

"As a matter of fact, I saw her driving through town heading in that direction about fifteen minutes ago."

Pulse jumping, he made his way to the door.

"Barrett?"

He turned.

"Why are you so interested in Shelby Arroyo?"

His face went hot, an unaccustomed feeling. Why was he interested? At that very moment, he could not come up with the words to explain it to himself or to her.

"No reason," he said.

"Okay. Betsy and I are looking forward to the Christmas Eve bash at the Gold Bar."

Christmas meant a lot to Ella, he knew. "We are, too. See you later." He felt her curious stare as he hastened out the door.

Shelby thought maybe she'd got the wrong directions, but the mailbox read 103 Lone Pine, which matched her Google search.

Ella Cahill told her Shep ran a tourist spot, though this didn't look particularly inviting. The small town was charming enough, every light along the main street twined with green garlands and pots of poinsettia plants clustered in front of the shops. Gold Country at Christmas time, perfect for a holiday postcard.

But Shep's place was a couple of miles out of town, set back from a road that could use some repaving. She saw no other vehicles on this lonely stretch. Peak season for folks looking for the gold mining experience was probably the summertime when they didn't mind splashing around in the cold water.

As she drew closer, she found a sign above the mailbox that read Gold Panning Adventures and Historic Gold Mining Museum. In the wide expanse of the front yard was a series of raised troughs and stacks of metal pans. There were no festive Christmas touches here.

Her temple throbbed, a sign that a migraine was still threatening. She hadn't helped things along by skipping breakfast in her haste to visit Shep. Her mother used to sneakily stow a granola bar in Shelby's bag before she left for her marathon school/work sessions.

In case you feel a headache coming on, she'd say. There would also be a couple of candy kisses there, too, in spite of Shelby's tirades about how she wanted to eat healthy. Odd. Her craving for a candy kiss at that moment was intense. She shook it off.

The office was a small wood-sided affair. At first she thought no one was home, until she noticed a glimmer of light from the side window. Hoping the proprietor would be more welcoming than Joe Hatcher had been, she approached the shop, letting herself inside to the jingle of a bell hung on the front door.

No one manned the small counter. "Hello?"

There was a cough from the back and a voice called out, "One minute."

Soon a man emerged, thin and tanned with a brown beard much fuller than Barrett's and a thermos in his hand. "Lookin' to try your hand at gold panning, miss?"

"Actually, no. I called earlier and left a message. I'm interested in your history museum."

His faint smile disappeared. "Oh, yeah."

"I was told you have some old maps and I'd love to take a look."

"Uh-huh."

She thought at first he had not understood her. "I'm Shelby." She decided not to provide her last name since that didn't seem to be earning her many fans in Gold Bar. He didn't offer his own name.

"Oh, I know who you are," he said. After a few seconds, he added, "I'm a good friend of Joe Hatcher's."

His face was as cold and hard as a rocky cliff. The hairs on the back of her neck went up. "I'm happy to pay for a ticket or something, in order to see the museum. I'm not asking for any favors."

"I won't take your money."

He said it as if her money was somehow dirty. She forced her gaze right back at him. "Shep, I'm here to see the museum. That is the point of a museum, to be seen, isn't it? I'm not going to cause any trouble. I just want to look at a few maps. Surely there's no harm in that."

He didn't answer.

A warm flutter of anger started up in her belly. "I don't have all day. Yes or no? Do I get in or not?"

Still the stony stare.

"All right. I'll leave." She went for the door. "And they say people in small towns are friendly," she grumbled. She had almost cleared the threshold when he called out to her.

"Down the path between the two pines. It's on the right. It will be dark inside, so turn on the lights yourself." Shep took his thermos and retreated to wherever it was he'd come from.

Still steeped in disbelief, she quickly headed down the path as directed before he had time to change his mind.

The museum was really just a long narrow building with a front and back door, which might have been a warehouse at one time or another. Now it was covered with aluminum siding and a sign on the front advertising Two Hundred Years of Gold Bar History.

She pulled open the door and it squealed as if it had not seen a can of oil in a few decades. The inside was ripe with the smell of dust and mildew, which did not bother Shelby in the slightest. Groping for the light switch, she found the area partitioned into smaller spaces by floor-to-ceiling screens that formed little rooms.

In the first area, she jumped when she saw what she thought was a man. It was a mannequin, dressed like a prospector, kneeling with a pan in his hands. Shep would probably have laughed himself silly at her fright. There was a display detailing the influx of would-be miners looking to strike it rich after James Marshall had made his historic discovery in the waters of the sawmill he was running with John Sutter. One man, one moment, had caused the entire country to go west.

She continued on toward the second partition, which was an overview of the various groups who gave up their domestic lives and headed in droves to the goldfields. People of all races and situations had joined the mad rush for the metal.

Shelby mused over the fake gold nugget on display for the museum goers. The geology geek in her marveled that gold was delicate enough to be hammered into the thinnest of wires and so versatile that it could be injected into the muscles of rheumatoid arthritis sufferers to ease their pain. The element was so rare that all the gold in the world could be compressed into an eighteen-yard cube and so common that every cubic mile of seawater contained twenty-five tons of gold. Plentiful and nearly impossible to extract.

The science of it never failed to awe her. In truth, it was the reason she believed in God. There could be no other explanation for the minute order of the metals, minerals and crystals she'd spent years studying. He was there in every minuscule detail, master creator, His signature in the gorgeous order of it all.

It puzzled her. Why would He so carefully create such marvels and yet allow His people, His most precious creations, to hurt each other so grievously? War, famine, abuse, neglect. If He was a loving father, why did He not intervene? And the most painful question of all? Why had he not helped Shelby see the truth instead of blaming her mother and making an enemy of the one person who loved her the most?

And the veins of gold she so eagerly sought for

her uncle? They would have to be pried out of the earth at great expense and trouble. For all its beauty, the quest for gold could be an ugly business. All the blood, death, sweat and toil that went into finding a paltry flake or two.

Her own emotions surprised her. Checking her phone, she was surprised to find that she had frittered away more than thirty minutes. "What's the matter with you?" Slipping her phone into her pack, she moved on.

The next room was exactly what she'd been hoping for. Set against the back wall was a map of California, hand drawn to reflect the territory as it was during the late 1800s. Underneath was a set of long, flat drawers. With eager fingers, she pulled open the top one, finding it full of maps of the stagecoach routes. The next drawer was a hand-drawn map of the nearby towns. Encouraged, she was about to open the bottom drawer which was labeled Gold Bar, Topo.

A sound brought her upright. The scuff of a shoe on the floor.

"Shep?" There was no answer but her own thundering heartbeat. She waited, feeling silly. Had she imagined the sound? *Just look at the map and get out of here.* She crouched down and grabbed the bottom drawer, just as Joe Hatcher stepped into view. Her body went cold.

He didn't say a word, just stared at her, hands behind his back.

She stared back, unwilling to let him see her fear, while her mind churned. He was blocking her exit from the small room. She could yell, but who would hear her? Only Shep, and he'd made his alliance clear. Her phone was in the small pack on her back.

Okay. She would stand up to him and do whatever was necessary to get out of there unharmed.

"What are you doing here?" she demanded.

He shook his head. "You are one stuck-up lady. What am I doing here? This is my town. I thought I'd stop and see my friend Shep. You're the stranger. Maybe you should tell me why you're here?"

"Visiting the museum. Isn't that what strangers do?"

His eyes glittered, the thick grizzled brows pulled together in a line. "You're trying to pull the topo maps. I figured that would be your next step. Still researching my mine."

"My uncle's mine."

"Didn't you learn, lady? You and Barrett stuck down there in the water, almost drowned? It ain't safe. All you're gonna get from investigating is a coffin."

"Thank you for your concern."

"For some reason, Barrett seems to feel responsible for you. Ain't you gonna feel guilty if he gets hurt traipsing after you?"

She remembered how she'd felt leaving him behind in the tunnel. "I'm not responsible for Barrett Thorn."

He stepped closer. She caught the tang of dried sweat on his body. "Hasn't your family done enough to Barrett?"

That guilt rippled through her like an earthquake. She recalled her uncle's words. *They hate me, they hate Devon, and for all their religious spouting, that will never change.*

"The Thorns don't want anything to do with me." Straight from Barrett's mouth.

"Funny how Barrett turns up where you are."

She was tired of being in this uncomfortable standoff. "I want to go, Mr. Hatcher. Let me pass."

He moved his hand to his belt and pulled out a knife. The blade gleamed in the low light. He smiled, stepped quickly forward and pressed the knife to her throat. She went still, paralyzed with fear.

Hatred simmered in his eyes, his breath hot and sour on her face. "What's the matter?" he grunted, the blade cold against her skin. "Scared?"

Yes, her gut screamed. "No," she said, forcing out the words. "Because you're not going to kill me here in your friend's museum, are you? That would be messy."

For a moment, his gaze flickered. She'd called his bluff.

Then he leaned in closer until she could see every crease on his weatherworn face, the sheen of crazy nestled deep in his eyes. The breath froze in her lungs.

He chuckled. "Sometimes life is messy, isn't it?"

ELEVEN

Barrett figured since he was in town, he might as well stop by the church and see if they needed any handyman help for the soup kitchen. The kitchen was Bree's brainchild, a biweekly offering of food to any in the area who needed it. Unfortunately, there were always plenty of hungry people. If Bree had her way, they would have offered food daily, but the small town didn't have the manpower or finances to make that happen.

The church folks were busy at the moment in a meeting, planning out the Christmas festivities, so he left without disturbing them.

His father picked him up after dropping off Brownie. They drove along in silence, Ella's question ringing in his ears.

Why are you so interested in Shelby Arroyo?

It made no sense. He had plenty to do. *Mind your own business*, his head told him. *Got sixty horses and a family to take care of.* Instead, he blurted out, "Dad, you mind taking the long way back, by Shep's place?"

"Got a sudden hankering to do some gold mining?"

"No, sir. I heard from Ella Cahill that Shelby was heading there and, uh, I just got this bad feeling."

His father nodded. "All right."

He was grateful his father did not pry further into his motivation, which he did not fully understand himself. He simply could not shake the sensation that she was about to step in a hole so deep she'd never get out. Something about her combination of earnest and stubborn attracted him like a bear to a beehive. *Attracted? No, just friendly concern, right?*

But why should he care, as Ella wondered? *Because you're supposed to care about your neighbors, even the ones that you have the most reason not to.* God made that pretty clear. Barrett settled back on the seat, his mind more at ease until they reached Shep's place.

His heart lurched to a halt along with the truck. Ken Arroyo's vehicle was there all right, and so was Joe Hatcher's.

"Be right back," he called to his dad.

"I'm here if you need me."

Barrett found no one in the office, so he jogged up the trail to the museum building. Throwing open the door, he ran inside.

"Shelby?" he yelled.

"Here," she called back. His lungs started working again. Was it his imagination or was her voice tight with fear? He ran toward her, finding her jammed in the corner of a makeshift room with Hatcher next to her, a knife in his hand.

Barrett stopped short, hands loose and ready, as if he was approaching a treacherous horse, angling his body between Hatcher and Shelby. "Put down the knife."

Hatcher gripped it tighter. "You tellin' me what to do now, too?"

"Trying to save you from doing something stupid."

"Stupid?" Hatcher's eyebrows raised to his hairline. "All I'm doing is what Shep asked." He pointed up to one of the flickering lightbulbs. "Needs to be changed but it's rusted solid in the socket. He asked me to come jimmy it out on account of his bad back, and that's what I'm here for." He sneered. "What did you think I was gonna do, boy?"

Shelby's face was dead white, her lips pressed tight together. "He put the knife to my throat, Barrett. He only stepped back when he heard you coming."

"She's lying."

"No, she's not," Barrett said, rage gathering like floodwaters. "You're going to jail."

Hatcher lifted a shoulder. "Well, it's her word against mine and the cops think she's nothing but trouble already."

Shelby touched Barrett's arm. "Let's go. I'll tell the police. We'll let them sort through it."

Barrett looked at her, puzzled. The spirit seemed to have gone out of her. Had Hatcher scared her that badly?

Hatcher grinned and lowered his voice as if he was confiding a secret. "Anyway, if I was going to kill you, you wouldn't even see it coming."

Barrett shoved him in the chest. "Get out."

Hatcher stumbled back, the knife still in his hand. "Watch yourself, Barrett. We ain't enemies yet, but that can change."

"I said get out," Barrett repeated. "Now."

Hatcher fingered the knife handle, and Barrett tensed, staying between him and Shelby.

Hatcher slid the knife back into the sheath on his belt and walked away without another word.

Barrett followed far enough to be sure the front door creaked shut behind Hatcher before he returned to Shelby. She was hugging herself, her curtain of hair gleaming like wet autumn leaves in the low light.

"We'll go to the police right now," Barrett said.

"He'll just talk his way out of it. It won't do any good." She squinched her eyes shut for a moment.

"You okay?"

She nodded, but he saw a ripple of pain cross her face.

"He didn't hurt you?" Barrett pressed.

"No, I'm getting a migraine headache."

"Uh-oh. Have you eaten today?"

A flicker of surprise showed through her discomfort.

"My brother Jack gets migraines when he forgets to eat or hasn't been sleeping well. It pretty much puts him down for the count if he doesn't take steps early on."

Her shoulders were sort of hunched, as if it hurt too much to stand up straight. "I'm okay."

But she didn't look okay, not by a long shot.

With a groan she bent to open the bottom drawer and let out a bitter yelp. "It's empty. Hatcher and Shep never intended to let me see the maps anyway. All this for nothing."

Hatcher had something to hide. Something big, big enough to draw Shep into the conspiracy, though Shep was probably doing his friend a favor without asking why. "They are putting a lot of thought into this."

She squeezed her eyelids together and rubbed her temples. "I'll figure out a way, but right now I can't think straight."

"Come on, we'll drive back to the Gold Bar and get you something to eat. I'll drive you in your truck back to the ranch."

"I can drive myself home."

"No offense, but no, you can't." She allowed him to take her around the shoulders. "Besides, you should come with me."

"Why?"

"You need food and I want to show you something."

He could feel the muscles of her neck, knotted like rope.

"Why are you here anyway?" she said.

"Dad and I were just passing through."

"I don't buy that, but my head is throbbing too much for me to grill you about it."

"Excellent, it will be a much nicer drive then."

He knew she must be feeling pretty bad since she did not even bother to fire off a retort as he led her to the truck and sent his father on ahead.

Shelby closed her eyes. Barrett was silent, which was a relief, since her head felt like someone had driven a spike through it, even though she'd taken a minute to swallow some of the migraine medicine she kept in her pack.

The feel of the knife pressed to her throat would not go away, leaving her muscles on high alert. She did not want to allow such a man to intimidate her, but she found her hands were shaking anyway, and not from the migraine.

Joe Hatcher may have intended to kill her right there in the museum. And he knew how to torture, too.

Hasn't your family done enough to Barrett?

She tried not to lean against Barrett's warm shoulder. *It's not like I'm asking him to take care of me.* Yet there he was again at the museum, and she'd been profoundly grateful to see him. Things might have ended differently if he had not come to her rescue.

She had no idea what it was that Barrett had to show her at the ranch, but the agony in her skull would not permit any deep thought. In a few moments, she found her head resting against his hard shoulder as the truck and trailer bumped them to Gold Bar Ranch.

Barrett took her hand and led the way into the quiet kitchen, which smelled of coffee and bacon. "Mom's run to the neighbor's, but there's always something to eat around here."

"I'm not hungry, really."

"Just a little bit in your stomach. Toast, maybe, with a slick of peanut butter."

She wanted to ask him exactly how much a "slick" was, but instead she watched through a cloud of pain as he toasted the bread, spread on a layer of peanut butter and presented it on a plate with a glass of milk.

She looked at him through bleary eyes. "Are you going to sit there and watch me while I eat?"

"Yeah."

"Can you at least eat something, too, so I don't feel like a zoo animal at feeding time?"

"Okay." He plucked an apple out of the bowl on the counter, took a big bite and sat down opposite her while she nibbled at the toast.

The bread was homemade and the peanut butter melted into a comforting ooze. She finished half before her stomach rebelled. "Thank you. That was great." The food helped, but her meds had not yet started to dull the agony.

He tossed his half-eaten apple into the bin and stepped behind her. His long fingers massaged her shoulders, gently kneading the tension away. Her head leaned back against his torso and she accepted his tender ministering.

"Does your brother get this kind of treatment?" she joked.

"Naw, but I take care of his chores for him when he's got a migraine."

Barrett was a gentle giant of a man, she mused. The kindhearted cowboy who would try to ease the pain of a woman whose family had devastated his own. Yet he couldn't forgive... But who could? Nobody, as her uncle told her.

"I really should go home, Barrett." She pushed away and tried to stand, clutching the edge of the table as sparks danced in front of her eyes. "I'm not good company."

He stood and took her hand. "Come with me."

Unable to resist, she allowed him to lead her to a small family room furnished with a worn sofa and a pair of rocking chairs.

"Sorry, we don't have a guest room because it's filled to the rafters with stuff for the Christmas Eve party, but you can lie down and sleep here until it passes," he said.

"Oh, I don't need..."

"Yes, you do." He grabbed a quilt. She sat on the sofa, eyes closed, trying to summon up the courage to walk herself out of the Thorn house. He knelt and pulled off her boots. Before she knew it, she was lying on the sofa and he was covering her up to her chin with a quilt that smelled of fresh air, as if it had been dried on the line.

"I don't want you to take care of me," she tried to say. "I don't want to need you, any of you." Instead, the warm comfort washed over her, the darkness soothing as he pulled the curtains closed, the whinnies of the horses outside blending into a lullaby.

In the corner of the room was a small tree, covered with silver ornaments and a hand-stitched tree skirt. The faint scent of pine told her it was real, probably cut down right here on the Gold Bar property. He bent and connected a plug, and a sparkle of delicate lights shimmered.

"There now. That's about right," he said.

"Barrett," she whispered, "thank you." But he had already left the room.

TWELVE

Barrett ordered his noisy brothers to hush up on account of their sleeping visitor. His mother looked particularly pleased to have a guest to fuss over and promised to give her a proper meal when she awoke.

"Jackie always likes a grilled cheese and coffee when he shakes off his headaches. I'll just see if there's more bread in the freezer. And I'm sure I've got some of that extra sharp cheddar left over."

Though Jack never corrected his mother, Barrett knew he did not enjoy her nickname for him. Still, it was good to see her smiling as he left her humming along to the ancient Christmas records she refused to part with. It reminded him how the ranch used to be a revolving door for visitors when Bree had been alive, especially during the holidays. His mother missed the bustle and the chance to exercise her gift of hospitality.

"I'm glad to see your smile, Mama," he said. He dropped a kiss on the top of her head before he headed outside to leave a message for Larraby and then muck out the stalls.

Owen caught up with him in the stables. "What's going on?"

"What do you mean, what's going on?"

"I mean, you're getting pretty tight with Shelby Arroyo."

"Not tight," he said. "Just being neighborly." He grabbed a shovel and went to work on the closest stable, scooping up mounds of soiled hay.

"Uh-huh."

Barrett stopped and faced his brother. "Uh-huh what?"

"Since Shelby blew into town, you two are together every time I turn around."

"That's an exaggeration."

"Is it? First you fish her out of the ravine, then you both are stuck in Hatcher's mine and now she's actually bunked on the sofa."

"Not bunked. She's sick with a migraine. Did you want me to leave her on the street corner?"

"No, but it all seems weird to me that she's suddenly welcome here, considering."

His jaw tightened. "Considering?"

"Come on, Barrett. Let's put it out there. Her cousin killed your wife and her uncle allowed it."

Anger flashed through him like white-hot lightning. "I know it, Owen. I'm crystal clear on the facts. It was my wife, remember? I have more reason to know that than you. If memory serves, you weren't even here when it happened."

He shouldn't have said that. It pained his brother that he had not been in the United States for the worst time in their family's history. And then the injury had left him a virtual invalid. Owen was born a protector. Barrett felt shame that he'd struck at his brother's vulnerability. He should apologize, but Owen was enraged.

His shoulders stiffened and he stood up to his full height, about an inch shorter than Barrett. "Yeah, I was somewhere else, wasn't I? Well, you know what I learned in Afghanistan? Two things, brother." He stabbed two fingers into the air. "One, never go anywhere without your body armor, and two—" his eyes blazed at Barrett "—know the enemies from the friendlies."

"Shelby loves her uncle, but she's not the enemy." When had he decided on that, he wondered?

"Yeah? Somehow I think her loyalties lie with another family, Barrett."

"Why is this your business?"

Owen folded his arms across his chest and looked down at his boots. "Maybe because I wasn't here, and now that I am, I want to do my part for the family…and you."

Barrett felt his ire drain away. His brother had fought his own battle and it followed him right back home to Gold Bar. "I get that."

"I don't want to see you hurt again," Owen said quietly.

Barrett blew out a breath and nodded. "Thanks. I know what I'm doing."

Owen looked at him long and hard before he nodded. "Okay. I'll trust your instincts unless I have reason not to." He turned and limped away.

Barrett put all his energy into mucking the stables, working until he was hot and sweaty in spite of the December temperatures. When the stalls were filled with sweet-smelling bedding, he checked on Swanny and tended to his other chores. By that time, it was well into the afternoon. He found Shelby and his mother on the porch, the Thorn family's old hound, Grits, sprawled on the bench between them with his head in Shelby's lap.

He laughed at the sight of Grits's eyes rolling in pleasure while Shelby rubbed his ears. "I see you've made friends with Grits."

"I miss having a dog." Shelby paused. "We took in a stray after my dad left. My sister and I named him Filbert and we doted on that dog until we had to give it away. We moved around a lot and most rental places aren't so dog friendly." Her fingers were slender and delicate as she soothed the fur. Grits let out a sigh that billowed his fleshy lips.

"How are you feeling?" Barrett said.

Her cheeks flushed a rosy pink. "Much better, thank you. I'm sorry to have been such a bother."

His mother waved a hand. "No, none of that. Happy to have you." She looked her son over. "You missed lunch, honey. Want a grilled cheese?"

Shelby giggled, a small dimple he had not noticed before showing alongside her mouth. "Your mother is a champion grilled cheese maker."

"You should see what she can do with a lasagna." He shook his head. "Don't need a sandwich, Mama, but thanks. I want to show Shelby some of Grand-dad's old things. Is that okay?"

"Of course it is." Her eyes danced. "You take your time and then she can stay for dinner."

"No, Mrs. Thorn. Absolutely not. I've taken advantage of your hospitality long enough. Besides, my uncle…" She paused. "Well, anyway, he's out of town and I need to keep an eye on things. Larraby is going to call and I want to have my thoughts together."

His mother looked slightly downcast. "Oh, well, if you change your mind, there's always plenty. I'm going to make chili and corn bread. The boys love it."

Barrett shooed Grits off Shelby's lap. "Let her up, boy."

Shelby stood and Barrett led the way along a shaded trail behind the ranch house. The air was cold, but she was zipped to the chin in her jacket, hair loose and dancing on the breeze. The sun glazed her fair skin and he was struck by the beauty of her face. Not so much the features as the passion that illuminated her from the inside, a kind of wonder at the path under their feet and the oak trees that towered above them.

"This place is gorgeous," she murmured, stumbling on a tree root because she had been eyeing a scrub jay. He reached out a steadying arm but she did not take it.

Message delivered. Jamming his hands into his pockets, he tried to clear his mind. The small cabin sported a coat of fresh ivory paint and deep burgundy trim. "Cheerful," his mother had declared when she'd chosen the color. "Just like Granddad."

He opened the door to the two-bedroom home where Granddad had lived for a decade after his wife had passed. They'd had talks about what it was like to lose your soul mate.

"Like when I lost my leg to the diabetes," Granddad had said. "It's gone but it still hurts like crazy."

"Does the pain ever stop?" Barrett had asked.

Granddad had gone quiet then for a while. "No, son. It dulls down to a softer hurt, but it never goes away."

Barrett's loss had dulled down to a softer pain, too, but now it was twirled together with a strand of guilt. Guilt that he could not forgive Ken Arroyo, as he knew Bree would have wanted him to. Guilt that he was more than a little attracted and preoccupied by a new woman? He gritted his teeth and quickened his pace.

* * *

Shelby gazed at the photos on the top of a scarred upright piano. She laid one fingertip on the family shot of all four boys, each clutching a fish they had caught. Barrett was the tallest even then, gangly, in his midtwenties, she guessed. Next to that photo was a picture of Owen in his military uniform, tall and proud, without the hostility she'd recently detected in his eyes.

"It must be something to have a family like this," she murmured. "All the old memories and history you share."

"Got plenty of stories, that's for sure. What about you? You close with your sister?"

She nodded. "I love her like crazy. I've almost sent her enough money to start on her training. She wants to be a nurse," Shelby said, pride creeping into her tone. "She's going to be a fantastic nurse because she's smart, determined, super detail oriented and so compassionate." She let loose a breath. "She got a lot of practice with our mom before we had to hire full-time care for her."

"Not doing too well?"

"She has dementia triggered by her stroke. There's a great care facility in Phoenix near where my sister will be going to nursing school."

"You ever see your mom?"

"Not as much as I should. I wish… I wish I had found out sooner that she was keeping the truth from me about my father."

She could see Barrett wanted to ask, but he probably didn't wish to come across as nosy. He stayed silent and she answered his unspoken question.

"He left us," she said simply, "and I thought my mother was the one that kept us from seeing him, that she was selfish and didn't want to share us with him." Moisture collected under her lashes. "I discovered last year when we had to pack up my mother's things that it was my father's choice, actually. He didn't want us. Part of why he left was that he never wanted kids."

Barrett shook his head. "I'm sorry, Shelby. That's a terrible thing to find out about your dad."

He could hardly conceive of it, she was sure. The Thorn family was as tight as any she'd known. "It hurts, but I can take it. The point is—" the confession dribbled out before she could stop it "—I was horrible to my mother about it and I never asked her to forgive me and now she doesn't even know who I am." Pain almost cut off her words. "It's too late."

"Maybe not," he said.

"What good would it do to apologize now?"

His eyes shifted in thought. "Well, Granddad said the hard stuff comes along to make us more like Jesus."

More like Jesus. It was an echo of her conversation with her uncle.

Barrett fixed her with a gaze bluer than the California sky. "Are you a believer, Shelby?"

The question startled her. "Yes," she said after a pause.

She could tell he was spooling the words out carefully. "Then maybe you should talk to your mother, not for what it will do for her, but for what it will do for you, for your soul, you know?"

"Maybe." Looking at his handsome face, chiseled and strong, she felt emboldened to ask a question of her own. "But if you believe that, Barrett, if you really believe forgiveness is for your own soul, then why don't you do the same with my uncle? Not for him, but for you?"

Emotions unrolled quickly across his face, anger, hurt, fear and last of all shame. "I... I can't."

"Then that doesn't speak well for your faith, does it?"

"No," he said, the word sounding strangled. "So I guess I should keep my advice to myself."

It got so quiet in the cabin she could hear the scuttle of a squirrel on the roof. She made a show of looking around the tiny spot. "Well, anyway, this is a nice place and I appreciate you showing it to me. I think I'd better go."

He yanked open a handmade wooden cabinet. "What I wanted you to see was Granddad's collection."

"His collection of what?"

Barrett unfurled a long cylinder of yellowing paper. "Maps," he said, finding a spot and pointing. "Look at that."

She hurried to see, her body brushing his arm. Her mouth fell open. "That's a rendering of the mine entrance on Joe Hatcher's property."

"It was Hatcher's father's at the time this was drawn, or more likely his grandfather's."

She peered closer, soaking in the faded details. "Wait," she said, peering closer. "This, this here. What is this?"

Barrett frowned. "I'm having second thoughts about telling you."

"Tell me, Barrett."

"It's a cave that Granddad said used to connect to the mine."

"Here? Right here on your land?"

"Not ours. The neighbor's. Oscar Livingston owns the adjacent property. He runs the Nugget Country Inn in town."

"Do you think he knows something about those red marks? Would he give me permission to access the mine via his property?"

"Maybe."

"Well, why didn't you tell me that earlier?"

"I forgot. The map didn't occur to me until I heard you were looking at Shep's museum. Granddad forbade us from ever sneaking over there and exploring because he said it was unstable and we'd be buried alive."

She caught his gaze. "Four boys and a forbidden tunnel? You tried anyway, didn't you?"

He looked sheepish. "Yeah, but he got wind of it

before we even made it out of the house and asked Oscar to bar up the entrance."

She felt like kissing him. Instead she grabbed him around the shoulders in a hug. He embraced her, and she marveled at the sheer muscle of his torso.

Elated, she moved to kiss his cheek but he shifted at just the same moment, so her lips grazed his. Electric sparks rolled through her.

A shadow flickered across the window and she jumped away from him.

"Uh, problem?" Barrett asked.

"I thought I saw movement, like someone was looking in the window."

He stepped away, clearing his throat. "I'll check. Stay here."

He went outside, returning in a few moments. "I don't see anyone."

She sighed. "I think I'm getting paranoid. I'm sorry."

"No harm done, but I'm showing you this map on one condition."

She hoped she didn't sound as breathless as she felt after the accidental kiss. Further, she hoped her cheeks weren't flushed red. *Business at hand, Shelby.* "What condition?"

"That you will promise me not to go down into that mine shaft alone."

"But…"

He raised a finger and glared at her. "No buts."

"But…"

"What did I just say?"

She glared right back. "Your mama wouldn't like you bossing me around."

"Well, I'm bossing anyway, and don't drag my mama into this."

She expelled a long, slow breath. "Okay. I promise I won't go down there alone."

"Good. So when do we go?"

She grimaced. "Hey. Just because I have to take someone, doesn't mean it has to be you."

His look was purely sarcastic. "And who else would be insane enough to head into an unstable tunnel with a half-crazy assayer besides me?"

The seconds ticked by. She could not think of a single person.

"Oh, all right. How about now?"

"How about no? I've got horses to feed and Mama said something about chili and corn bread. She would be mortally offended if I wasn't here to eat it."

"Fine, tomorrow then, and no fair dragging your mama into this if I'm not allowed to. Did you get your cell working after it got doused in the mine?"

"No. It was ruined. Using my old one. You?"

"Borrowing one from Uncle Ken. Give me your number so we can connect about a time."

She punched her number into his cell and he did the same with hers. He offered a smug smile that she found irresistible. "But it's still not fair."

He lifted a careless shoulder. "My mama, my ranch, my rules."

"You're one stubborn cowboy."

"So sue me," he said, returning his granddad's map with a chuckle.

THIRTEEN

Shelby was practically giddy as she drove home and fixed herself a peanut butter sandwich. Another entrance to the mine meant she would not have to fight Joe Hatcher anymore. She could take her samples without his consent or cooperation. The weight she'd been carrying around dissipated in a cloud of relief.

Curiosity kindled afresh. Those red marks she'd seen in the mine tumbled through her thoughts. With unfettered access to the mine, she could find them again and decipher the message they were obviously intended to deliver.

The sandwich was a far cry from Mrs. Thorn's chili and corn bread, but she did not want to risk spending any more time than necessary with Barrett.

The man befuddled her, plain and simple. He awakened trifold feelings: attraction, though she hated to admit it; anger, that he was so free with spiritual advice and so reluctant to take his own; and pleasure when she was sharing time with him. How could all of those feelings coexist? Black-and-white, that's how she liked things, and Barrett represented all the millions of shades in between.

The easy solution was to cut him out of her life, yet she found herself depending on him at every turn. It was simply maddening.

She liked him, or was it more than simple fondness?

No, it's not, you ninny. Focus on the anger, she told herself. *You're here for a job and that's it.* Barrett was bossy, a hypocrite who did not have the right to tell her what her soul needed when his own was far from spotless. She wanted to dismiss him outright, but his words continued to turn in her mind, twirling like a single leaf clinging to a winter-blasted tree. *Then maybe you should talk to your mother, not for what it will do for her, but for what it will do for you, for your soul, you know?*

It hadn't occurred to her that the act of asking for forgiveness was as important as the forgiveness itself. Maybe Barrett was right, because the change in her Uncle Ken from the man she'd known in her younger years was dramatic. He used to be loving, softhearted, but now his eyes burned hollow and hate filled, poisoned from within.

I am not guilty of anything but loving my son, and I will never seek forgiveness for that. Not from God and not from Barrett Thorn.

Her uncle's rage, Barrett's hypocrisy, her own inability to face the mother she had wronged. All three of them were caught in deep tunnels of despair, like veins of gold imprisoned in stone.

"God," she started, "help me to fix things with Mom."

Far from eloquent, it was the first prayer she'd uttered about her relationship with her mother in a very long time. The words were rough, as if they had lingered too long in some abandoned mine shaft.

"God, help me," she repeated, louder, insistent. There was no answering feeling of comfort, no dawning certainty about what to do.

Her thoughts were interrupted by Larraby's phone call. It was clear from his tone that he thought she was making up or exaggerating her encounter with Hatcher. It was a relief to end the call.

Darkness filled every corner of the house, so she turned on a few lights and played some Christmas music on her phone: Bing Crosby, Tony Bennett, Burl Ives, all her mother's favorites. She opened the newest issue of *Geology Today*, which would normally enthrall her, but she found she could not concentrate on the articles.

It was as if her heart longed to be somewhere else. The smell of the cozy quilt and the twinkle of the lights in the Thorn family room felt so very far away as she lay down on the couch and pulled on a blanket until her senses were finally overcome with sleep.

* * *

Shelby sat up with a start, disoriented, heart thumping. Her cell phone told her it was after midnight. The house temperature had dropped because she'd forgotten to set the thermostat.

She blew on her fingers as she tried to figure out what had awakened her. Tiptoeing to the window and pulling the curtains aside, she looked out onto the front lawn, but there was no sign of any visitors. Across the drive, the land dipped away and the roof of the barn and stable was barely visible.

Uncle Ken had downsized considerably, but he still kept Diamond, an older mare named Pattycake and her beloved companion, Buddy. The three were stabled for the night since Diamond was finicky about being in the rain and Pattycake and Buddy had grown used to nighttime stabling with their previous owners.

A flicker of movement caught her eye. Diamond's coat gleamed in the moonlight as she trotted away from the stable. How had she got free? Had Zeke been careless about securing the animal?

Shelby considered. The pasture was fenced and Diamond could stand a night out in the cold since the temperature would not drop below freezing. Even if Shelby chased after her and offered an apple, Diamond's favorite treat, there was no guaranteeing the headstrong horse would come when summoned.

High-spirited indeed, as Barrett had said.

"You're on your own then until morning, you stubborn horse." A moment later her worry shifted to the other two. How would Pattycake and Buddy do, wandering at night with another storm threatening? What if Zeke had simply not stabled any of them for some reason?

With a sigh, she pulled on a pair of boots and a jacket, grabbed a flashlight from the kitchen drawer and shoved her phone in her back pocket.

As the weatherman had promised, rain had begun to fall and she eased her hood over her head. At least her migraine hadn't made a return appearance. She flashed on the sensation of Barrett's strong hands kneading comfort into her tense shoulders.

"Can't you keep him out of your mind for five minutes, Shelby Elizabeth Arroyo?" Yanking up the zipper so hard it caught her chin, she strode toward the stables.

Back in the more profitable years, Uncle Ken had built a lovely wood-sided barn with adjacent stables that could accommodate ten horses, securing them comfortably in roomy stalls that opened up onto the main pasture. Most of the stalls were empty now, except the three on the end for Diamond, Pattycake and Buddy, who needed to be within hearing distance of each other. Normally two powerful lights mounted on the exterior of the stables would be switched on, but at the moment they were not.

Zeke had not done his job, apparently. She hastened into the barn, nearly tripping over a small can of red paint and a broom, shining her light on the control panel. The switch that controlled the exterior lamps was already in the on position. Figuring a circuit must have popped, she moved it to the off position and then on again. Nothing happened.

She turned on the interior barn lights, and the lamps set high into the ceiling flickered to life. Uncle Ken had not replaced the ones that had burned out so it was scant help, but it provided her enough of a glow that she felt more confident. "Must be some kind of a problem with the exteriors only."

Flashlight ready, she headed to the stalls. Her shoes crunched on the wet ground as she drew nearer. Beaming her light at her feet, she realized she was stepping on broken glass from the exterior lamps. Several feet away was another pile of shattered fragments, the remains of the other lamp. One broken lamp might be a bizarre accident, but two wasn't. A chill snaked up her spine.

She switched off the flashlight and melted as quietly as she could into the shadows. Sweat beaded her brow when she detected the low squeal of someone opening the door of the farthest stall. She heard Pattycake's soft nicker of surprise.

The person wore a black coat, and Shelby caught no gleam of hair, which indicated that whoever it was wore a ski cap.

Whoever? She knew exactly who it had to be. Joe Hatcher.

What he was doing in the stables she had no clue,

but it was meant to hurt, of that she was positive. Creeping backward, Shelby inched around the side of the stable, yanking out her phone and shielding it with her shaking palm in case the light could be seen.

Someone's here in the stables, she texted Barrett. But it was almost 1:00 a.m. He would not be awake. There would be no help from Barrett and the Thorns. She could not call the police from her hiding spot because the stranger would overhear. Gripping the phone, she tried to keep her breathing steady and silent.

She needed a weapon. Uncle Ken kept a shotgun in the house and he'd taught both her and Devon how to use it. Would she remember? Could she actually pull the trigger? *Get somewhere safe*, her mind screamed. The house was her best option. From there she could call the police and defend herself.

Fear gripped her so tight she was paralyzed. "Move, move, move," she silently commanded her body. After a slow count to three, she sprinted toward the house, not daring to look back. She would not be able to hear the sound of pursuing feet over her own frantic breathing.

Go.

Stumbling over clumps of soaked grass, she fell, rocks biting into the knees of her jeans. Scrambling to her feet again, she ran faster than she'd thought possible, not bothering to undo the pasture gate, instead clambering up and hurtling over the top rail. Splinters jabbed into her palms but she did not slow her pace until she exploded through her uncle's front door.

Slamming the door closed, she turned the bolt and sucked in precious lungfuls of oxygen. The police call took only a moment to place, but she knew it would be twenty minutes or more before they arrived at her uncle's place. Until then, she would be her own defender.

She pounded down the hallway and retrieved the shotgun from the closet and the shells from the shelf. She slid a round in the chamber and slid the action forward. Then she loaded the remaining rounds into the magazine.

Returning to the front window, she drew aside a corner of the curtain. The view was quiet, undisturbed. Shrouded moonlight glistened on the wet grass with pockets of deep shadow in between. She could not make out the barn. Needing a higher vantage point, she jogged upstairs to look through her uncle's bedroom window.

At first, she saw nothing, just darkness and rain. Then an orange spot flared into her field of vision. Her brain did not make sense of it for several moments. The orange spot danced and grew, shooting up in ragged tongues, obscene in the blackness.

Fire.

The stables were on fire.

She could not breathe, could not move. She imagined Joe Hatcher holding a lit match to the clean hay, watching while it caught, observing the mounting terror of the trapped horses, listening to them die. He would be smiling, enjoying the pain and misery.

Rage unlike any she'd ever known enveloped her in a white-hot grip. A rush of adrenaline lit her from the inside out.

"I will not let you murder those animals," she hissed in a voice she did not even recognize.

Shotgun over her shoulder, she yanked open the front door. Sprinting, she raced back to the stables. The smoke was pouring from the end stall where Pattycake and Buddy stabled together. She yanked open the door, shotgun ready, but there was no sign of an intruder, only the terrified horses.

"Don't worry," she murmured to the panicked animals. "I'll get you out." She eased around them to gently prod them toward the door when a shadow of movement made her tense. She had only enough time to hold her arm up, but the blow caught her on the shoulders, knocking her to the floor beneath the horses.

Covering her face, she tried to avoid being trampled and shield herself from further attack.

There was the sound of the stable door swinging shut and the scrape of a wedge being kicked under it.

She crawled toward the door, head down to avoid the thickening smoke. Pressing her palm against the wood, she confirmed what her instincts already told her.

She was locked in.

FOURTEEN

Barrett didn't bother saddling a horse. He gunned the engine on his truck, tires churning up grit as he took the road to the Arroyos' property. Owen was in the passenger seat, tight jawed and silent, a rifle across his lap. He'd been awake in the kitchen, the perpetual victim of pain and insomnia, when Barrett had staggered in.

"I'm coming," he'd said. "You need backup."

Barrett had not argued.

Leaves torn loose by the incoming storm slapped against his windshield, the wipers keeping time to the panicked beating of his heart. Someone in the stables?

"Police are en route," Owen said. "She reply to your text?"

He shook his head. Would Shelby play it smart and stay locked inside as he'd advised, no, ordered, in his text? Would he, if the situation was reversed? If he thought someone was threatening his horses, he'd grab his gun and charge out like an angry bear. Any of his brothers would do the same.

The rain sheeted on the glass, his headlights picking out pockets of water collected on the road. He had to slow a few times when his tires caught in several potholes, jarring them both. The house came into view, some lights showing on the bottom floor.

They cut to a hard stop behind Ken Arroyo's truck. The smell of smoke hit them immediately, the crackle of flames jerking their attention toward the barn. "The stables are on fire."

"I'll get the horses out," Owen said. "You see if Shelby's hiding in the house like you told her to."

Owen disappeared into the night. He was a crack shot, a trained soldier, and he had way more experience with this kind of situation than Barrett. Barrett made it to the front door in moments, stomach plummeting when he found it ajar. He pushed it open with his boot.

"Shelby?" he called softly. Then louder. No answer. The eerie stillness of the house telegraphed the truth. She'd done what he would have. Gone to save her horses. He texted his brother. Shelby's at the stables. Coming now.

Then he ran, flat out pounded down the sloped drive and onto the graveled trail that led to the stables. Drifts of smoke filled his nostrils. He found Owen trying to unjam the door at the end, but the wedge was driven too deep.

"Let me," he said, grabbing an ax and striking at the hinges. It took Barrett a half dozen chops to knock away the metal. He hauled open the door. Owen went for the horses when a shot exploded through the air, sending him to his knees.

"Don't touch my horses," came a faint voice from the corner.

"Shelby?" Barrett yelled, smoke stinging his eyes. "Don't shoot. It's Barrett and Owen. We're here to get you out."

Crouched in the corner, she looked at him, peering through the smoke. After a moment, she struggled to rise but crumpled back into the hay. He gathered her up and carried her to the barn, laying her down while Owen tended to the horses.

She lay on her side, sucking in air, coughing. He brushed the hair from her face. "Easy does it. Just focus on breathing."

She sucked several more lungfuls before she struggled to sit up.

"The horses are out," he soothed. "Just stay put until we get an ambulance here."

She sat up anyway. He felt a thrill of relief. "What happened?" he asked, figuring he could keep her still for a while if she was talking.

She coughed violently. "I saw someone setting a fire in the stables. Whoever it was knocked me down and locked me in."

"Hatcher?"

"It had to be."

Barrett frowned. "Did you actually lay eyes on him?"

"No," she admitted. Her face was smeared with black streaks. "But I know it was him."

"So you came to stop him? With a shotgun?" Barrett was incredulous.

"It stopped your brother, didn't it?"

He almost laughed out loud.

Shelby was not smiling. "The horses would have died. Diamond was loose before I got here. I was trying to let Pattycake and Buddy free when he locked me in." Her expression darkened into a mask of rage. "He was going to let the horses burn alive. What kind of monster would do that?" Her lip trembled, just a little, and he could stand it no longer. He wrapped her in his arms and pulled her close. She pressed her face into his shirtfront and he knew she was trying desperately not to cry.

"It's okay now," he whispered. "It's okay."

She gulped and sniffled and he breathed in the comfort of her presence, the knowledge that she was safe, and pressed his lips to her hair. She raised her head, tears staining her cheeks.

He carefully wiped them away with his thumbs. Her skin was satin soft, warm, and he cradled her head between his palms, easing away the shivers, the fear.

"How could anyone do that?" she said so softly he could barely hear her. The eyes that met his were tortured, cut through with a pain he desperately wanted to ease.

"I don't know, honey." He let his palms cup her cheeks. "But the important thing is you're okay and the horses are all right."

She raised her head to his, and without thinking he pressed a kiss to her warm mouth. For a moment, her lips melted into his and his soul felt an ease that he had not experienced since his wife's death. The feeling was so intense it startled him and he drew back, staring.

"I, uh…"

She pulled away and stood. "I have to go find the horses. They're scared."

He regrouped, trying to shove away the reality of what had just happened. "You should wait to be checked out by the paramedics."

"No. I'm okay." She headed toward the pasture.

"I'll help."

Owen met them outside. "Stables are clear of any intruders and the horses are uninjured as far as I can tell, but we'd better have Doc Potter check them over. I got the fire mostly contained, but I'll keep working on it." The sound of sirens pierced the night. "Cops are finally showing up."

"We're gonna take a look at the horses." Barrett hoped his voice didn't sound strange, but Owen just nodded.

"I'll stay here to keep more water on the fire and brief Larraby when he comes."

Shelby grabbed a few apples from the barn and several lead ropes.

Barrett was struggling over what to say when she stopped short. "There they are. All three of them."

The horses were gathered under a dripping oak. Diamond gleamed as if she had been carved out of marble. She tossed her mane when she saw Barrett and Shelby.

"I think Pattycake and Buddy will cooperate, but Diamond might be tough." Shelby handed him two apples. "Can you get them while I try to coax her?"

Barrett agreed. Shelby was right. The frightened horses were only too happy to nibble their apples and allow themselves to be fastened to lead lines. They followed him back to the stables eagerly enough. There was still the stink of smoke in the air but it was quickly dispersing in the wind.

The two did not want to be parted, the smaller gelding whinnying pitifully when he tried to stable them separately. Barrett put them together in an undamaged stall, stroking their trembling sides. He dried them down and gave them water and oats, talking softly until they settled.

Larraby had finished with Owen by the time Shelby had returned, wet to the boots, with Diamond.

"Miss Arroyo," Larraby started.

She shook her head. "I'm taking care of this horse first. Then I'll answer your questions."

Barrett hid a smile at the look of annoyance that

crept over Larraby's face. Owen's expression said he was enjoying it, too.

"Quite a woman, isn't she?" Larraby said in an uncomplimentary tone.

Yes, Barrett thought with a growing sense of awe that scared him. *Yes, she is*.

Shelby was only half paying attention to the police officer's questions.

Barrett's kiss had enflamed her already amped emotions. Why would he do such a thing at such a time? And more significantly, why did his kiss make her feel like the tight bands holding her heart together had sprung wide open? Out of control. That situation must not be allowed to continue. There was no future with Barrett, a man who despised her kin and distracted her from her duty to save her uncle. She squeezed her hands into fists and brought her thoughts into focus.

"So are you going to go arrest Hatcher?" she demanded.

"I will question him and if he can't provide an alibi, then we'll go from there." Larraby shoved his pen in the pocket of his rain slicker.

"He's guilty," she said.

"Yeah, but we got this little thing called 'innocent until proven guilty' here in this country and you didn't witness him committing a crime." Larraby looked at Barrett and Owen. "Can either of you make a positive ID?"

The brothers shook their heads. "No," Barrett said, "but that doesn't mean she's wrong."

"Doesn't mean she's right either," Larraby said. "I'll take some pictures and look for prints." He walked off.

The horses, Shelby thought with a start. Would Hatcher return to try again? How would she protect them?

Barrett seemed to read her thoughts. "The horses should come to the Gold Bar until your uncle returns." He paused. "And so should you."

"I..." She took a breath. "I would appreciate it very much if you could take them for a few nights in case that monster returns, but I'll be fine here." The thought of staying in the empty house all alone made her skin crawl, but she could not, would not, impose on the sympathy of a family who hated her uncle. Besides, the less time with Barrett, the better.

Barrett glowered. "Not safe."

She held up the shotgun. "I'm a pretty good shot. Ask Owen. He can confirm."

"Well, my head is still attached to my shoulders, so I guess that's something," Owen said, clicking off his phone. "Jack and Keegan are on their way with the trailer. We'll get the horses settled in at the Gold Bar."

She nodded. "Thank you. I am grateful and my uncle would be, too."

"I doubt that," Barrett muttered.

She straightened. "I'm going back to the house

to call him. Thanks again for your help." She hurried away a few paces.

"I'll walk with you," Barrett said.

"I don't need an escort," she tossed over her shoulder.

"Yes, you do."

She turned to face him. "Look, Barrett. It's…it's just not a good idea for us to be in close proximity."

"Probably not."

"Then why are you still following me?"

"Dunno." He wiped the rain from the brim of his hat.

"Yes, you do. Tell me." Her face went hot, remembering the kiss. He seemed to read her thoughts.

"Yeah," he sighed. "I don't understand why I…" He looked up at the watery moonlight. "I mean, considering my feelings about your uncle and all…" He stopped again. "But I can't stop thinking about you, and you make me feel, I dunno…" He shoved his hands in his pockets. "Awww, never mind. Forget I said that. I'm comin' at least until you get inside and lock your door, so that's that."

She didn't know what to do but force her legs into motion while her mind reeled. *Can't stop thinking about you…?* How could he possibly have put into words the same emotions flailing around her insides?

It was ludicrous, dangerous, ridiculous.

Keep walking, Shelby. Just keep walking.

Mercifully, Barrett did not speak at all on the

way back to the house. By the time they got there, Shelby had herself firmly under control.

"Thank you, Barrett. I'll come for the horses as soon as my uncle gets back. We'll pay you to board them, of course."

"Naw, you won't."

"Yes, we will. You don't want to do a favor for my uncle."

He grimaced. "Could be God's giving me the opportunity to change myself." A soft sigh escaped him. "I hate it when He does that."

She could not help giggling at the plaintive look that showed through the weariness. There was just something about the guy, the way he struggled with his faith, yearned to do the right thing in spite of the flaws that got in his way, that made her want to kiss him again.

"Anyway," he said. "I'll see you tomorrow."

"Tomorrow?" She blinked hard. "Oh, right. Our mine expedition."

"Yup," he said. "And don't even think about going without me. I…" He cleared his throat. "I know I upset you tonight with that kiss and all my crazy chattering, and I apologize. It won't happen again."

His gaze was firmly fixed on his boots.

"It's okay," she said softly. "It was just a kiss and some words. No harm done."

He looked at her then, something wild and wounded and yearning in his expression. "Yeah," he said. "No harm done." He turned away.

"Barrett," she called.

He stopped.

"You aren't by chance planning on sleeping in your truck and keeping an eye on me tonight, are you?"

His eyebrows shot clear up to his hairline. "Me?" His tone dripped with innocence. "Why would you accuse me of such a thing? I'm not a stalker, you know."

She knew, and she also knew that was exactly what he intended to do. She opened her mouth to complain when he waved her off.

"Go on now. Starting to rain again and I'm getting cold."

"I thought you were too stubborn to get cold."

"Must be turning weak or something."

She smiled, taking in his proud form, tall and strong, as if he defied the rain to fall on him. Not weak, not anything close to it.

The door was ajar, as she'd left it in her haste to protect the horses. The smell hit her first. As she flipped on the lights, it took a moment for her eyes to adjust to the darkness.

She screamed.

FIFTEEN

Barrett bolted through the open door, almost plowing into Shelby from behind. Blood oozed down the walls, dripping in scarlet rivulets to the wood floor. No, not blood, his brain corrected. The chemical scent of paint permeated the space.

Shelby was staring at the wall. Written in the paint was a message: You'll Die. By the time he had the presence of mind to take out his cell phone and photograph the horrible phrase, the letters had smeared and dripped, drying in ugly trails, yet still shouting out their message of hate.

You'll Die.

He put a hand on her shoulder. She was trembling under his touch.

"I saw the can of paint at the barn," she whispered. "While you and I were securing the horses, he came up here and did this."

Barrett did not know what to say. Ken Arroyo's living room was desecrated. The man did not deserve that, no matter how Barrett felt about him. Nor did his niece.

"I'll get Larraby," he said, anger humming through his veins. "And when we're done here, you're staying at the Gold Bar. Period." His tone brooked no argument and she did not offer one. That worried him almost as much as the fact that whoever had gone after the horses had been at large here, too.

Would Hatcher actually do such a thing? Barrett couldn't fathom it.

His phone call summoned Larraby and another officer who began printing and photographing. At the end of the process, they allowed Shelby to try to clean up the spilled paint before it dried on the floors. Barrett helped, but they succeeded only in smearing the color over the walls and in bright arcs across the wood planks.

"I'll leave an officer posted out front to keep watch tonight," Larraby said, his tone more conciliatory than it had been earlier. "You can call him if you feel uncomfortable."

"No need," Barrett said. "She's coming to stay at the ranch."

Larraby mulled it over. "Okay. We'll schedule some drive-bys to check on the property anyway."

Shelby called her uncle. Barrett stepped outside to allow them some privacy while she packed an overnight bag and he phoned his mother.

"Can we accommodate a houseguest, Mama?" he asked after he filled her in.

"You have to ask?" she scolded. "I'll put some clean sheets on the bed in Granddad's cabin. She'll be snug and safe as anything there."

Perfect, since Barrett's bedroom window looked directly out on the cabin.

"And when Ken gets home," she said firmly, "we will help him clean up the mess properly."

Help Ken. The idea would have disgusted him a week before, but now it did not feel quite so distasteful. "Yes."

"You know," she said softly. "God's going to work good out of this. I can see it happening in you."

In him? God had to be pretty amazing to work good out of the present mess with Shelby. Was it possible he could rid himself of his long-simmering rage and forgive, not for Ken's sake but for his own? It would be a tall order, very tall.

"Be home soon, Mama."

Shelby locked up the shotgun, pulled the front door closed behind her and secured it. "Uncle Ken is going to try to catch an earlier flight, but he still won't make it home before Monday afternoon. He's really upset, of course, but he's appreciative that your family is looking out for me."

Appreciative. Little did Ken know that Barrett was intrigued by his niece to the point where he could think of nothing else. Odd.

Maybe he should be feeling guilty about having such strong feelings for another woman, but he knew Bree would want him to find another partner. She'd told him as much on one of those long summer nights when they'd sat on the porch, talking and watching the fireflies paint the skies over the ranch. She was unselfish like that. But to love someone whose uncle enabled his son to kill Bree? How could God mean for that to happen?

God's working good out of all this. I can see it happening in you.

With an effort, Barrett pulled himself back to the reality of the situation. Problem solving, the soothing list of things to be done, details to work out. That's what he craved.

He mentally worked through the logistics of housing three extra horses, who to ask about how to clean paint off Ken's hardwood floor and how to structure his chores so he could be sure Shelby did not go sneaking off into the mine without taking him along. He did not like the angry glint to her eye and the set to her chin. If Hatcher intended to scare her off from her explorations, he'd missed the mark by a mile.

Something odd and primal pulsed in Barrett's stomach as he pulled into the Gold Bar property. He had the feeling that he was bringing Shelby to the place she belonged, his home, his world, as if she was his woman, his soul mate. It was the way he had felt about Bree, that she was his and he would do anything in the world for her, anything at all.

Struck motionless by the thought, he stared out the window, the truck idling in the front drive. She reached out her hand and cupped his fingers in hers.

"I feel like I'm trespassing."

"No," he said softly. *I wouldn't want you anyplace else,* he wanted to add, but he'd already made a fool of himself one too many times that day. "You're welcome here. Don't think anything different."

She gathered up her purse while he hopped out and opened the passenger door for her. His father had the front door ajar before Barrett made it there.

"Shelby, I am so very sorry that this is the kind of treatment you've got from Gold Bar. It's beyond comprehension."

To Barrett's great surprise, Shelby started to cry. Tom Thorn, who was strong enough to fight for his family and love a complete stranger, folded her in an embrace.

"It's going to be all right," he said, patting her back. "When you're staying here, you're an honorary Thorn and nothing is going to happen to you. I guarantee it."

Barrett saw Owen, Jack and Keegan standing behind their father. Their faces showed varying degrees of emotion: Jack complacent, Keegan enjoying the whole spectacle and Owen reserved and still suspicious. He knew all three of them would honor their father's words and protect Shelby Arroyo, no matter their own feelings.

Pride mingled with his confusion. God made

something special when he put the Thorn family together. He watched his mother draw Shelby inside, no doubt to try to tempt her into eating something. He busied himself with fussing over the horses, who didn't need it, and checking the supply of hay, which was more than adequate.

When his mother was finished, he walked Shelby to Granddad's cabin. His mother had left the lights on and turned down the bed. She'd even placed a plastic-wrapped plate of Christmas cookies on the table.

Shelby sighed. "Oh, I wish she hadn't gone to the trouble."

"Trouble? You made her whole holiday season, and this way Keegan won't eat the entire batch all by himself."

Barrett went to the corner and plugged in a string of lights, illuminating the small tree that had been in the family room. Shelby gasped, the lights reflecting in the pools of her eyes.

"There was no need to move it here for me," she whispered.

"Like Dad said, you're an honorary Thorn, and that means you get the full holiday treatment."

He made sure the windows and back door were locked, just for extra good measure.

"Good night, Shelby."

"Good night." Her voice was soft and tender.

Though he wanted to look back and see her silhouetted in the lamplight, he forced himself to keep walking, distancing himself from feelings that his heart could make no sense of.

Shelby was up with the sun, alerted to morning by the soft sounds of ranch life. Peeking out the window, she caught her breath at the sight of Barrett forking flakes of hay down into his truck to deliver to the waiting horses. His breath steamed in the cold air. He worked alongside his brother Jack.

The lights were on in the ranch house where she imagined Evie was busily preparing breakfast. Shelby dressed quickly, tying back her hair and swiping on a quick brush of mascara and lip gloss, chastising herself as she did so.

Who is this vanity for? Barrett? You're not going to be a couple, get that through your head. Her head was not the problem, unfortunately. It was her heart that did not want to listen to the list of reasons why Barrett was an unsuitable match. The list was compelling enough.

First, there was the problem of her uncle and their mutual familial hatred. If that wasn't enough, Barrett had obviously been desperately in love with his wife and he was simply confusing a mild attraction with something deeper. Furthermore, she had no intention of staying around after the mine was properly assayed. Aside from visits to her Uncle Ken, she had plans to open her own assayer's office in Arizona where her sister was attending school, close to their mother.

Her stomach clamped tight at that thought. There were so many things she should say to her mother, things which would not be received by the woman who no longer even remembered who Shelby was.

She realized she was standing as frozen as a statue, while her mind ran rampant. "Get it together," she hissed at herself, pulling on her jacket and yanking open the door.

Barrett and Jack looked up as she strode purposefully toward the stables.

"Good morning. I thought I'd check on Diamond and her partners in crime."

"We've got them in the western pasture by themselves for now. They were skittish after their eventful night." Barrett peered at her as if wondering if she felt the same.

"I'm going into town," she announced, "to talk to Oscar Livingston about access to the mine."

"I'll go with you," Barrett said.

"No need."

"I've got to get some brackets to put the tables together for the Christmas Eve dinner and your truck is still at your uncle's place, so why don't you hitch a ride with me?"

Why? She'd just given herself three good reasons why. "But…"

Barrett was talking to his brother.

Evie called from the house, "Time for breakfast."

Shelby wanted to flee, but how could she face that smiling woman and turn down her gracious hospitality? Feebly, she followed Jack and Barrett into the kitchen.

The scent of sausages and scrambled eggs made her mouth water. Tom greeted her with a cheerful smile. Evie gestured her to a chair and poured coffee into mugs at the wide table. The wood bore the scars and nicks from generations of people who had gathered around it over the years.

Shelby imagined the little grandchildren that would come along one day, sitting at that same table, hunched over coloring books or learning to roll out piecrusts like Grandma Evie. Her own childhood had been punctuated by moments like these, until their father left. Then it was as if a darkness had settled over the family, in spite of their mother's desperate attempts to lighten it.

The anger had gradually taken over Shelby's soul, and with it a need to punish the person she felt was responsible, the wrong person. Her father did not want the children he had made. She should be brimming with rage at him, shouldn't she? But she found she was only filled with sadness at what she had lost, the years she could never get back.

Did the Thorns understand what a precious thing they housed between the old ranch house walls?

She looked at Barrett, Evie, Tom, and she knew the answer was yes. They had all endured great sorrow at the death of Bree and they knew how fragile a blessing could be.

Owen and Keegan joined the group, cheeks ruddy

from the cold morning. Before she knew what was coming, Barrett had taken one of her hands and Evie the other. The brothers completed the circle and Tom said a simple grace. The company broke into a lively conversation about ranch duties.

Evie dished up a plateful for Shelby. "We're going to the evening church service tonight, honey. You're invited, of course. They added that service for those ranching types, who have plenty of early chores."

"Or just can't get up in the morning," Owen said, laughing at Keegan who was in midyawn.

"Thank you," Shelby said, trying to figure out a way to politely decline. She feared it would be awkward, downright painful, to attend church with everyone's eyes on her, the whispers about the newcomer whose life had been threatened on a regular basis.

"Meg at the church said she could use more pickles for the soup kitchen's Christmas Day luncheon," Evie said to Barrett.

Keegan laughed. "Better start rationing. We're down to the last fifteen cases."

"Funny," Barrett said. "You're just jealous because you don't know how to cook anything but toast."

Jack startled Shelby by speaking. "He doesn't know how to make toast either."

She joined in the laughter, marveling at how the levity buoyed her spirits and pushed away the fear from the night before.

She was halfway through her eggs when there was a knock at the door. Jack admitted Officer Larraby, who declined the offer of coffee and breakfast. He looked ill at ease in the Thorn house. Shelby's nerves went taut as she waited for him to report his findings.

"I came to let you know that Hatcher has an alibi for last night."

Shelby dropped her fork. "I don't believe it."

"His daughter, Emmaline, says he was home all night."

"She's lying because she's scared of him," Shelby said. "He's a tyrant."

Larraby shrugged. "Possibly, but his truck engine was cold, hadn't been driven."

"He could easily have come on foot," Barrett put in. "It's not more than a mile to Ken's place."

"He wasn't the least bit wet when I spoke to him. Hair dry, coat dry on the rack, boots dry, too."

"So he changed, dried his hair," she said. "You can't possibly think he's innocent."

"It doesn't matter what I think," he snapped. "My job is to enforce the law and there's no evidence to arrest him. No prints at your uncle's place, no tire tracks, no eyewitnesses and nothing to refute his alibi."

Barrett threw down his napkin. "How about all the threats he's made to Shelby? The knife he pulled on her at the museum? Guy's clearly out to get her."

"Like I said, not enough," Larraby said, moving toward the door.

"When will it be enough?" Shelby said. "When I'm dead?" The words dropped like bombs in the quiet kitchen.

"We'll keep digging," Larraby said. "I'll let you know if we come up with anything. Sorry to interrupt your breakfast."

"Where's his ex-wife?" Shelby blurted.

Larraby blinked. "What?"

"I heard in town from a waitress at the coffee shop that his wife, Cora, left him almost five years ago."

"Yeah, I'm sure the gossips loved that whole drama. What does it have to do with the present situation?"

"Emmaline said Cora was an amateur geologist, that she'd spent time in the mine. When Barrett and I were down there, it was clear that someone had done some exploring, left some marks behind."

"That mine is more than a hundred years old."

"The marks were recent."

"I still don't see where you're going with all this."

"I wondered if Cora would be willing to talk to me about what she saw down there. It might explain why Hatcher is so reluctant to let me in. Maybe he knows there's a rich vein of gold and he wants to keep it for himself."

Larraby shook his head. "Sounds like you're cooking up some wild theories."

Shelby stared at him. "What happened at the stable last night was not my imagination. I'm going to find out who is responsible, with or without your help."

Larraby folded his arms across his chest. "We're investigating and I'm doing my job."

"And I'm going to do mine, also."

"You do that, Miss Arroyo, but whacking on the hornet's nest by prying into Cora's life is asking for trouble."

"They're divorced. He doesn't get to decide who Cora talks to anymore."

"She chose to leave Gold Bar and as far as I know, she never looked back."

"Yeah," Shelby said, thinking of her own father. "Well, maybe it's time she did, whether she wants to or not."

"Like I said, if you mess with the nest, you're likely to get stung, but I can see my advice is falling on deaf ears so I'll go about my business." Larraby departed, the door slamming shut behind him.

Shelby realized everyone in the kitchen was now staring at her.

"I'm sorry. I think I've ruined your breakfast."

"No," Owen said, his blue eyes so like Barrett's. "But Larraby does have a point. Hatcher's divorce is his business."

"My horses almost burned to death and there's a threat painted on my uncle's living room wall, so

I'm not so concerned about Hatcher's feelings at the moment."

Owen's face was contemplative rather than hostile as she got up from the table. The men stood to be polite, a gesture which made her blush. Still courteous in spite of the trouble she had brought right into their midst.

Barrett caught up with her outside.

"Ready to head to town?"

She arched an eyebrow. "I didn't think you'd still want to be involved with a woman who's whacking a hornet's nest." She'd thought he'd smile, instead his face was dead serious.

"Like Dad said, you're an honorary Thorn. Thorns stick together, even when we disagree."

She swallowed. "Your brother Owen might not accept that."

"Owen has his own battles to wage. This family is all he has left and he'll fight to the death to protect it."

"Seems to me like that would describe all four of you."

He nodded. "Yes, ma'am. Now, are you ready to go?"

"Yes."

"All right. I just gotta load a case of pickles into the truck."

She smiled as she watched him go. For some reason, she'd been provided the comforting shield of the Thorn family.

You'll Die. It was a threat she could not allow to spread to Barrett and his kin. She would risk her own life for her uncle and the truth, but she'd make sure no danger would fall on the Thorns.

SIXTEEN

Barrett delivered the pickles before he picked up the boxes of brackets and a dozen folding chairs that the hardware store owner loaned out on a regular basis. Shelby helped him load the chairs into the bed of the truck, though he didn't want her to.

"Chivalry is nice and all that," she said, as they slid the wood in the back, "but four hands are better than two and my hands are pretty strong."

He had no doubt of that. Across the street from the hardware store was a thrift store with colorful dresses and handbags displayed in the window. Shelby's attention was caught and he followed her gaze.

Emmaline was exiting with a shopping bag. Shelby hastened over, Barrett following.

"Hi, Emmaline," Shelby said.

The woman shied like a startled colt. "Oh, hi."

"Doing some Christmas shopping?" Shelby asked.

Emmaline shrugged. "Not really. I just needed a plain apron so I can add some holiday trim. There was a skirt, too, I've been admiring with this really pretty beading along the hem. I love fancy clothes even though I have no occasion to wear them."

The sadness of that statement tugged at Barrett's heart. "You're coming to Christmas Eve at the Gold Bar, right?" Barrett suggested. "That's an occasion if I ever heard one. I even wear my best jeans, the ones without the hole in the knee."

She offered a tentative smile. "Imagine that." She twisted the handle of the bag. "Um, I know you probably want to talk to me about the thing that happened at your uncle's place. The police did, too. I told them everything. My dad was at home with me and I'm not going to talk about it anymore no matter how much you pressure me." She clamped her mouth closed.

"I understand," Shelby said. "I'm not going to ask you to speak out against him."

Barrett was surprised. He admired Shelby for not trying to force the girl to possibly betray her father.

"I have something else to ask you. I wondered if it might be okay for me to contact your mother."

Emmaline's mouth dropped open. "My mother?"

"Yes. You said she liked to explore the mine. I wanted to ask her about her observations and if she knows anything about the marks down there."

Emmaline's gaze dropped to the ground. "My mother's gone. She left us when I was in high school. Mom and Dad are divorced."

Shelby touched her very gently on the shoulder. "That's hard. I understand."

Emmaline's eyes glittered with anger. "Oh, really? You understand how it feels when your mother leaves you? When you're not a big enough reason for her to stay?"

"Not my mother, my father."

Surprise flickered through Emmaline's anger. "Oh," she said. "Well, anyway, I don't know where my mother is. I wouldn't know how to find her."

"Can you tell me her last known address? Any family members she might have contact with?"

Emmaline shook her head. "No. As far as I'm concerned, I don't have a mother anymore."

Barrett wondered if Shelby felt the same way about her father. How unutterably sad to lose someone who was still walking the planet. What a waste.

"I didn't mean to upset you," Shelby said. "I'm sorry."

Emmaline gathered her bag close and blinked hard at the tears that had formed under her lashes. "It's okay, but please don't talk to my father about it, all right?" Her tone was pleading. "He can't think straight about her. He goes a little crazy when her name is brought up, so I've learned not to mention it."

What kind of life did this girl have with a mother who abandoned her and an unbalanced father?

"I won't," Shelby said, and Emmaline looked relieved.

"We'll be sure to save a seat for you on Christmas Eve." Barrett hesitated.

Emmaline laughed. "Don't worry. I know what you're worried about, but my father never goes to any gathering. You don't have to be concerned about him showing up." She held up the bag and smiled brightly. "But I'll be there with a fancy new skirt on. Well, new to me anyway."

"Emmaline," Shelby said. "I heard that you were really attached to Diamond before she was sold to my uncle."

Emmaline bit her lip. "Yes. She is the most beautiful horse I've ever seen. If she were mine, I would never have sold her. Ever. I can't understand how my mother could do it. Even my dad didn't want to sell Diamond because he knew how much I loved her, but they were my mother's property." A look of disgust curled her lip. "That's how she saw Diamond, as property. We both begged her to keep the horse but she wanted out, out of ranching and out of our lives."

Christmas carols played softly in the store behind them, at odds with the tragic story unwinding on the sidewalk. Barrett wasn't sure what to say but he wished he could think of something. Words eluded him, as they often did, but Shelby broke the silence.

"Why don't you come by and ride Diamond sometime? She needs more exercise and my uncle wouldn't mind."

Her brows shot up. "Really?"

"Sure. It would be good for Diamond."

And good for Emmaline.

"Um, okay. Maybe when my dad is away. He wouldn't like it. He doesn't like me to do anything that reminds him of my mother."

"Whenever you'd like. Right now, Diamond is at the Gold Bar, but in a few days she'll be back home." Shelby gave Emmaline her cell number. "Text me when you want to come and I'll be sure there's somebody there to help you."

Emmaline nodded. "Okay. Thank you."

Shelby stood watching Emmaline walk away, coat collar pulled up to her chin.

"That was a nice thing you did there," Barrett said.

Shelby continued to gaze in the direction Emmaline had taken until she disappeared among the throng of people stringing lights along the eaves of the Grange Hall. "I understand how she feels."

"Maybe you can help her process what happened with her mother."

"I've got to figure out how to process my own situation first." Her smile was rueful, but he saw a touch of hope there, and it lifted his spirits. "Anyway, I'm itching to talk to Oscar Livingston. If your granddad's maps are accurate, there's a way in from his property."

"All right," he said with a sigh. "Let's go."

The Nugget Country Inn was a picture-perfect Victorian house set on the edge of town, backed by a rugged stretch of foothills that gradually gave way to the Sierras. The meticulously painted two-story building boasted quaint gingerbread trim twined with lighting for the holidays. The small lobby was warmed by a crackling wood fire and guests sat on plush settees and chairs, enjoying mulled cider and gingerbread cookies.

Shelby breathed in the scent of the spices and the decked-out fir tree crammed in the corner of the room.

Oscar Livingston was behind the counter, an enormous man as tall as Barrett and three times as wide. His full white beard was at odds with his perfectly bald head.

"Welcome," he boomed. "Morning, Barrett."

"Good to see you, sir," Barrett said, returning the man's vigorous handshake.

"Brought a pretty guest, I see. Can I get you a mug of cider, miss?"

"I'm Shelby Arroyo," she said. While she craved the offered cider, she decided it was best to keep things businesslike. "No, thank you for the cider, even though it smells delicious."

"Arroyo?" He mused. "Ah. Ken's niece."

She held her breath but did not see any ill will creep across his broad face at the mention of her surname. "Ken is proud as peas about you. Tells everyone who will listen about his niece, the assayer."

Her cheeks warmed. Uncle Ken was her father and her uncle all rolled into one and how good it felt to know she'd made him proud. *And I'm not done yet*, she silently reminded herself. "That's nice to hear. Actually, I've come on assaying business. I'm surveying the mine for my uncle."

"I heard you were taking a look on Hatcher's property." He cocked his head. "Didn't take it well, did he?"

"No."

"He's making things more difficult than they have to be," Barrett put in. "So we're looking for another way."

Oscar nodded, a frown wrinkling his forehead. "Oh, I get it. You want to access the mine via my property."

"Yes," Shelby said. "That's exactly what I want."

The phone rang on his desk, an ancient rotary model in a shade of avocado green. "Excuse me just a minute." He listened and then called to the back. "Hazel, can you come here a minute, sis?"

A large woman with the same full cheeks and warm smile stepped out of the back room. "Well, hello," she said. Bypassing the counter, she planted a kiss on Barrett's cheek and extended a plump hand to Shelby. "I'm Hazel Livingston and I see you've met my big brother."

Oscar chuckled. "She's always happy to remind folks that she's two years younger."

"Girl's gotta hold on to her youth," Hazel said.

"How's Shannon?" Barrett asked. "Coming home for Christmas?"

Hazel beamed. "Shannon's my daughter," she explained to Shelby. "She's studying in New York. Premed. Can you imagine that? Premed, and her mama never even went to a day of college."

"Her uncle neither," Oscar put in. "Too bad she's probably not coming back for Christmas." He gave Barrett a sideways glance. "But since she's not, uh, maybe we'll come to the Christmas Eve dinner, if we can get free. We'll bring pie."

Barrett laughed. "Pie would be great. I'll tell Mama." He paused. "You know, if Shannon does make it home, it would be okay for her to come, too."

Hazel twisted up her mouth. "Oh, no. We wouldn't want to make Jack uncomfortable."

Shelby read between the lines. Shannon and Jack had a tumultuous past. Life in a small town might be harder than she thought with everyone knowing everyone else's business.

"Folks in the Hickory Room need more towels," Oscar said. "I'll just go bring them up while you watch the front, okay? Be right back."

Hazel nodded as Oscar slipped away. "He's good to me." She pointed to her leg, which Shelby now noticed was a prosthetic. "Lost it to diabetes last year. Don't know what I would do without Oscar." A guest approached the desk and Shelby and Barrett stepped aside to allow Hazel to take care of her customer.

Shelby felt restless at the delay. To pass the time, she perused the enormous collection of photos

mounted on the side of the enclosed spiral stair-
case. They ranged from black-and-white snapshots
to modern colored ones, showing the parade of
guests that had spent time at the inn over the last
fifty years, she estimated.

"There's a lot of history here," she mumbled.

"For sure," Barrett agreed.

As she scanned the collection, her attention was
caught by one in particular. "Look," she said, grabbing Barrett's arm and pulling him closer. He bent
to look.

"It's Joe Hatcher, and that must be his wife, Cora,
next to him."

Hazel had come over to join them, leaning on a
cane for support. "Yes, they spent their honeymoon
here right after they got married."

"Do you remember Cora?" Shelby asked. "What
was she like?"

"Yes, I remember her. She was an elegant woman
with lovely clothes and jewelry. I remarked to Oscar
what an unusual couple they made since Joe is such
a homespun kind of fellow."

Shelby took another look at the tall slender
woman in the photo. Cora Hatcher was indeed elegant, her hair done in a soft chignon, handbag
matching her pumps. "Do you know where Cora
went after the divorce?"

"I don't really know."

Oscar returned. "Hazel, it seems these youngsters

want to go exploring the mine using the entrance on my property."

Hazel's face blanched. "Oh, no. You can't do that."

"Why not?" Shelby said.

Hazel shook her head, fingers pressed to her mouth. "It's dangerous. People have disappeared, young people, doing just what you're proposing." She looked as though she might cry.

Oscar stroked his beard and patted her soothingly. "One of our guests about three years ago was a prospector at heart. Young kid, college boy, name of Charlie. Had the gold fever pretty bad. We warned him not to go down into those mines, and of course I forbade him from going on my property. He went missing. Some boards were loose that I had nailed over my entrance so the cops searched the tunnels, but they never found him. We figured he went exploring, found a way into the mine, fell down one of those shafts and broke his neck or something."

Hazel gripped her brother's arm. "Don't say it. I can hardly bear to hear the words."

Oscar stroked her hand comfortingly. "We searched every spare minute. His family came out, too, clear from Nebraska. They were broken up and there was never any resolution for them. Terrible, never to know what happened to your son."

"Yes," Shelby agreed, suppressing a shiver. "That is terrible."

"So you see," Oscar continued, "that's why I can't allow you into that mine, not today or ever. I'm real sorry."

SEVENTEEN

Not even Shelby's persistent arguing would sway Oscar from his decision. He shook his head firmly, chins wobbling. Finally, Barrett led Shelby outside, Oscar following.

"Please reconsider," she tried one more time. "I promise I will be careful and I won't go down in the mine alone. Barrett's agreed to come with me."

He shook his head. "I'm sorry. Risking two lives is worse than risking one. I can't allow it."

She took his big hands in hers. "Mr. Livingston, this mine may be the only thing standing between my uncle and bankruptcy. If I can't get in through your entrance, I will have to have the police force Hatcher to comply, and I believe he's already tried to kill me to prevent that from happening."

Oscar gaped. "What? That's...that's hard to believe. Why would he do such a thing?"

"I don't know, but someone wants to keep me from doing my job." She told him about the death threat written in paint and the fire in the stable. Her voice wobbled once, and Barrett wished he could embrace her.

"Please," she said. "Your entrance is the safest way."

Oscar stroked his beard. "Let me think about it." He took down Shelby's cell number. "I'll call you tonight with my decision, okay?"

Shelby thanked him profusely and they returned to the truck.

"Well, all I can do now is wait," she said.

Waiting was not her strong suit, Barrett knew. Judging by her fingers twisting together and the frantic tapping of her foot on the floor, evening was going to be a long time coming.

Having tried unsuccessfully to get Shelby to attend church with the family, Barrett had to settle for insisting she lock herself in the cabin with old Grits for company.

As added insurance, he made sure the two younger dogs, Ida and Pockets, were on patrol. Ida was a border collie who would do nothing more than try to herd any strangers into manageable groups, but Pockets, the German shepherd, was protective of the property. Both of them would raise a ruckus if anyone approached who was not a member of the Thorn family or a long-time ranch hand. He double-checked that her cell phone was charged and his number programmed in.

"Phone is working. Go already," she said. "I'll be perfectly fine."

Of course she would, and it was not like she was his kin or even his sweetheart. But why did his concern for her safety gallop first and foremost in his thoughts?

"'Cause you're losing your mind," he muttered to himself, earning a look from his mother.

"What, honey?"

"Nothing, Mama," he said, helping her on with her coat as they got into the truck.

Still, he worried through the service as he sat and tried to listen to the pastor's message. The tiny church was decorated with pine boughs he'd personally cut at the Gold Bar. The creative ladies in the congregation had twined little white lights around the branches and added scarlet ribbons. He wished Shelby was there to see it.

It was astonishing to him that this woman whom he had fished out of a ravine not even a week ago had changed his life, like it or not, and made him face head-on his most uncomfortable feelings. *What's happened to me?*

When the service was over, he left his brothers to shuttle their parents home after the coffee-and-cookie hour was done, while he drove back to the ranch faster than was legal. It was almost eight thirty when he rolled up the drive, and the skies were clear, spangled with a brilliant carpet of stars.

The lights were on in Granddad's cabin and Ida and Pockets greeted him with wagging tails. A good sign that all was well, Shelby was safe. He breathed out an enormous gust of air. Then Pockets stiffened, tail erect and ears swiveling. Both dogs let out an earsplitting round of barking before they tore around to the back of the cabin.

He sprinted after them. The dogs continued their crazed barking, circling through the dense coyote bush that served as a backyard to the cabin. Their intensity told him something was hiding under those bushes. Or someone? Twigs crackled as he pushed forward.

A light shone behind him. "What's going on?" Shelby stood with a flashlight, shivering in the cold. The dogs ran to her, barking, before they about-faced and dived once more into the bushes.

"Go back in the cabin," he said. "There's something out here." He didn't wait to see if she complied, but grabbed an ax from the woodpile and charged into the bushes himself. Wet leaves slapped at him, snagging his shirt. He pressed on, shoving through the foliage, lifting the lower branches with his ax to look underneath. A heavy bough snapped as he lifted it, and whatever was underneath rocketed out.

Claws scrabbled against the bark of a knotty pine tree.

The dogs went wild, lunging and scratching. A

raccoon peered angrily down from a branch, eyes showing red in the night.

"All right," he said, exhaling. "That's enough, dogs."

Reluctantly, the dogs broke off their frantic search, trotting back over to Barrett, their mission ended. He shouldered the ax. He was about to say something when he noticed an impression in the mud underneath the side cabin window. The outline was blurred. Might it be a partial footprint? Before he could examine closer, the dogs barreled across the wet ground, obliterating the print.

"Was it an animal?" Shelby said.

Were the raccoons solely to blame for upsetting the dogs? Or was it possible that someone had been spying through the window? His mind was beginning to see danger everywhere. No need to spread his paranoia to her. "Raccoon." His eyes met hers. "You're cold. Let's get you inside."

She allowed him to usher her back into the cabin, and she sat shivering on the sofa. He closed the curtains and fetched a quilt from the closet, draping it around her, then started a log burning in the fireplace. Grits lumbered over and eased his way onto the cushion next to her. She stroked his droopy face.

"It's unlikely anyone would be able to get onto your property undetected, right?" Shelby said. He wasn't sure if she was comforting herself or him. "Just coyotes and raccoons and things."

"Sure." His gut was not nearly as convinced, but

he had no proof. When daylight came, he intended to make a more thorough search, in case the raccoon wasn't the only thing prowling the night around Granddad's cabin. He sat and faced her. "What if Oscar says no?"

She cocked her head and drew her slender legs up underneath her, tucked her hands into the long sleeves of her sweater. "He'll change his mind. I'm sure of it."

"But if he doesn't and there's no other easy way in? After hearing what Oscar said about that college kid, are you willing to possibly risk your life over this thing?"

"It's not just a thing, Barrett," she said, hugging her knees. "I wasn't exaggerating about my uncle's financial position. He needs this mine to work out."

Barrett felt the old familiar anger at the mention of Ken. "He'll land on his feet," Barrett couldn't stop himself from saying. "He'll sell some property and bail himself out."

"He's already spent most of what he had trying to help Devon."

Anger flashed through him. "Helping him avoid prison was expensive, huh? Maybe if he'd have stopped enabling his kid to escape responsibility, they'd both be better off." The words flew out like poison-tipped arrows. He breathed deep, trying to get some control.

She stared at him and he could see his own ire reflected in her eyes. "He lost his wife," she said.

"Me, too," Barrett growled, wishing immediately that he hadn't, but the floodgates were open. "Did you know that I fished Devon out of a ditch two months before the accident? He was drunk, wrecked his motorcycle. I took him home, talked to your uncle. Told him he ought to make sure the boy was straightened out before there was real trouble."

"I didn't know that."

He scrubbed a hand over his face. "Know what your uncle did to punish him? Bought him a car to replace the motorcycle."

He heard her expel a breath. "Aunt Opal, his wife, died in childbirth after losing five babies to miscarriages. I know it's not an excuse, but Uncle Ken tried to be everything to Devon that he'd lost, to fill up the holes. He made mistakes. He knows that." Her voice broke.

"We all make mistakes," he said, "but a real man takes responsibility for them. Devon has tried to do that and he's still practically a kid, but Ken can't face the fact that he failed as a father."

She took his hand, her fingers silk soft on his roughened ones. He wanted to pull away, but he couldn't.

She gazed into his eyes. "I thought a real man was one who could forgive." She hesitated. "Like Christ did."

He sighed heavily, his inability to beat his own anger defeating him. "I'm nothing like Christ."

"Both your mother and my Aunt Opal would

probably have said that's the point, that we're supposed to become more like Him, through all the troubles and tragedies."

He squeezed his eyes shut. "I can't." He felt her hand caressing his cheek and he kept his eyes closed in hopes she would not stop.

"I'm not sure I can either," she said. He opened his eyes to find her kneeling in front of where he sat on the couch, expression so earnest it took his breath away. "But I… I'm going to go see my mother and say the things I should have said earlier, even if it doesn't change anything."

"What made you decide to do that?"

"Being here, with your family. Seeing what my mistakes have cost me."

He looked into her jade eyes, so rich and deep, and he wanted more than anything to say that he could forgive Ken Arroyo. But the hard stone in his heart would not be broken, and it had taken the place of the soft flesh that used to beat there.

"I am glad for you," he said.

She wanted more, and so did he, but he could not give it. Her hand fell away and he realized the truth. His anger was a mountain between them that could never be crossed. He'd followed God all his life, he knew that he should do what God demanded of him, but he was too wounded, too weak.

He got up, shame weighing him down like a rock-fall. "I should go." She walked him to the door, standing on the porch. He was torn with the intense desire to leave, yet his feet would not let him.

Her phone buzzed and she answered. Barrett was grateful for the distraction. He gazed up at the stars, hands jammed in his pockets, trying to accept the gulf that lay between them, that always would.

When she disconnected, her smile was jubilant.

"Oscar said yes. He'll meet us at the entrance at 6:00 a.m. tomorrow morning."

He nodded. At least he could help her find the answers in the mine that would put her life in order, and maybe Ken's, too. If that was all he could offer, so be it.

"Dogs will keep watch tonight and I can look over your cabin from my window. I probably won't sleep much, so text me if you hear anything. I'll see you in the morning," he said. He let himself out of Granddad's cabin and trudged back to the house.

Shelby kept her focus on the task as she packed supplies into her backpack and double-checked that she had extra flashlight batteries and some food and water just in case. The memory of her conversation with Barrett intruded anyway.

Ken lost his wife.

Me, too.

In those two words, there was such a flow of hurt that had hardened over the years like igneous rock. In his voice, she'd heard the underlying message. He was unchangeable, immovable, frozen in his pain and unforgiveness, just as Uncle Ken was frozen.

"Lord," she said, squeezing her eyes shut. "I don't deserve to ask, but please help them both out of this darkness."

The prayer did not dull the edge of her unhappiness, but for some reason it felt right to say it, just as it had the moment she'd told herself it was time to go and see her mother. Would unburdening herself before her mother change anything between them? No, but perhaps it would change something inside Shelby's soul.

More like Jesus.

Her breath came out in a rush. Like Barrett, she had a long way to go.

The sky was dark, the horses munching their morning meal, when she let herself and Grits out of the cabin. Grits lamented their early departure with a low moan and a full body shake that sent his long ears whirling around his snout.

"I know, sweetie," she said, giving him a pat. "But the early dog gets the bacon, right?"

Grits did not look convinced as he trotted off toward the main house.

Barrett showed up wearing a Giants baseball cap.

"No cowboy hat today?"

"Don't want to lose a second one," he said. The words were light, but his eyes did not have their usual sparkle. He wore hiking boots and a jacket, a small pack over his shoulder. He sported his usual style of shirt in a different color and she hid a smile. She'd seen him exploring the ground around the perimeter of the cabin, and his scowl told her he was unsatisfied with whatever he had or had not found.

"Did you get breakfast?" she said. "There's time if you want to grab something."

"No, I'm okay. Let's get this over with."

Over with. The phrase stuck in her ears as they headed up the road. A wall was up between them now, and it was clearly Barrett's desire to keep it that way. Grief cut at her heart. He was right. The only thing left to do was get the job done so they could each go their own ways. She tightened the straps on her pack and quickened her pace.

It was much faster to hike to Oscar Livingston's property than to drive the truck, so they took a narrow path cut through a grassy hillside.

Barrett finally broke the silence. "I told my brothers and Dad what we're up to. If for some reason they don't hear from us by noon, they'll come running."

"Good to know."

"Keegan really wanted to come, but he's working with a new horse today. He's kind of unpredictable."

"Keegan or the horse?"

"Come to think of it, both of them."

They walked the rest of the way in silence until they let themselves through the gate onto Oscar's property. Since Oscar lived at the inn, the small house was empty, showing signs of wear and weathering. The land itself was overgrown with tall grasses on the low, flat plain, which eased down into a gorge peppered with old, gnarled trees poking out at odd angles.

Oscar waved a meaty hand, the other clutching two hard hats, which he presented to them.

"Got lights on them, too, so you don't brain yourself hopefully."

"Thank you so much, Mr. Livingston."

"Call me Oscar."

They put on the hard hats and Barrett shoved his cap into his back pocket.

Oscar led the way to a wood-framed entrance, wedged into a scrubby hillside on the near side of the gorge. It was boarded over, but the plywood was beginning to rot, the rusty nails popping free from the wood. Oscar handed Barrett a crowbar.

"Here you go, son. Better your strapping young back attacking this thing than mine."

"Yes, sir," Barrett said. It did not take him more than five minutes to pry loose the boards. The black maw of the mine opened before them. A ripple of excitement raced up Shelby's spine.

Oscar put a hand on each of their shoulders, his face troubled. "I have a bad feeling about this, and so does Hazel. Is there any way I can talk you out of it?"

"No, Oscar, but we'll be fine, I promise."

"You both need to be careful, extra careful."

"We will," Barrett said, and Shelby nodded her agreement, pressing a kiss to Oscar's round cheek.

He shook his head. "I'll just never forgive myself for what happened to that young fella, Charlie. I wonder sometimes if I had just been stronger with him, told him louder, forbidden him from going prowling around this place." He shuddered as if the frigid air from the mine had chilled him. "That hunger for gold," he said, "can get a person dead."

You'll Die. The memory dripped like blood through her thoughts.

You won't scare me off, Hatcher. No one will.

She squeezed Oscar's hand. "Nothing will happen to us, I promise." She turned toward the entrance and Oscar gripped Barrett's arm.

"I'm old-school, son," he said. "In my day, a man looked out for a woman's safety."

"In my day, too," Barrett said.

"Okay, then. You bring her back safe and sound."

"I will, sir."

"All right. I have to go help Hazel with the breakfast service. We still haven't got cleaned up from yesterday's Christmas tea, even though she hired on extra help. Hazel works too hard unless I'm there to share the load, but I will come back when I can."

Barrett nodded, shaking hands with Oscar as if they were concluding a business meeting.

Shelby was grateful that Barrett still intended to keep her company, in spite of the distance between them. With Barrett right behind her, Shelby switched on her headlamp and eased into the crypt-cold darkness.

EIGHTEEN

The hard hat was not comfortable, but Barrett figured it was better than getting bashed on the skull again. He tried to edge up in front of Shelby, but true to form, she led the way.

The mine had obviously been worked at one point. Busted-up tracks indicated there had been a system to move carts back and forth.

"The rails were for the ore cars," Shelby said, as if she read his thoughts. "They must have found a workable vein here. The miners would dig out the ore and haul it outside where it was put through a crusher to extract the gold."

He breathed in a damp lungful. "Air seems okay."

"They dug a shaft for ventilation and to release any dangerous gases."

"How do you know that?"

She grinned. "I spent the wee hours poring over your granddad's maps. There's one that shows the entrance and the shaft. That's about it."

"Sketchy."

"Yep, but that's the fun of it, right?"

He shook his head. "If you say so."

"Actually, reading the topography, I'm guessing this shaft connects to Hatcher's somewhere north of here. If we follow these tracks, I'm sure we'll get there."

"Does your uncle own the mineral rights to this whole area?"

"No, mostly just what lies under Hatcher's property, unfortunately."

Barrett was secretly relieved. If Arroyo wound up in the gold mining business, at least he wouldn't disrupt Oscar's land, too.

Shelby was busily taking pictures and writing notes on a spiral pad. He stayed quiet, allowing his vision to adjust to the gloom. The entrance was no more than ten feet high and maybe twice that wide. A rusted, overturned ore car lay on its side and something, he suspected rats, rustled in the recesses of the space.

At least the floor was dry and for that he was grateful. It was his mission to get them both in and out with no more plunges into icy underground lakes. He noted the timbers wedged into the rock to support the overhead portions of the tunnel. "So what's the shelf life of a support beam?"

She joined him in examining the wood. "I don't see much in the way of rot. Fortunately, it's dry and you don't get termites down here."

Awesome. At least they didn't have to worry about bugs.

His light caught on a metal box covered with dust. He could read enough that his heart skipped a beat. "TNT," he said.

She stared. "Reminds me that someone tossed a stick at me shortly after I arrived in this town."

He nodded, stomach muscles tight. "I remember."

"Barrett?"

"Yeah?"

"Those boards came away pretty easily from the entrance, didn't they?"

"Yeah."

"As if they could have been removed and then nailed up again, wouldn't you say?"

"I might."

"As much as I hate to admit it, someone could have grabbed themselves some TNT from this mine, instead of Hatcher's."

"Or a million other places. This is Gold Country. The place is riddled in every nook and cranny with leftovers from the mining industry."

"The dynamite, those red marks in the tunnel and the mysterious disappearance of Charlie, Oscar's guest at the inn. What's going on in Gold Bar, Barrett?"

"I wish I knew." Then again, maybe he didn't. Just keeping her safe was all he could think about.

She grew quiet as she stepped past the dynamite and followed the tracks. "Okay. It's six thirty already. We'd better start moving if we're going to get in and out before the Thorn cavalry arrives."

They crept into the narrow tunnel, and he had to hunch to keep his hard hat from scraping the rock. No need to generate any sparks, he thought uneasily. Debris covered the floor along the rails so they had to step carefully to avoid twisting their ankles.

She stopped, beaming her lamp at a patch of rock that looking like nothing special to Barrett.

"What? Something sparkle at you?"

His comment caused her to chuckle. "I'm looking at the quartz veining here in this fracture."

Her index finger traced something that must be significant, though it looked like more rock to his ignorant eye.

"Not gold?"

"No, but it can be a good indicator." She pulled a hammer from her pack and began to whack off some rock chips, which she slid into a heavyweight bag. The sound echoed and boomed down the tunnel. "Certain elements are telling, too. Arsenic, antimony, mercury, selenium, thallium. It's like being a detective, in a way. The lab will give us the final verdict."

He whistled. "Well, you certainly got the smarts for this job, I'll say."

He thought she might be pleased by his compliment, and that made him feel good.

"Thank you. I studied hard every moment and

worked two jobs, but I still couldn't have done it if my uncle hadn't paid most of my tuition."

Her uncle. Somehow they always came back to him. It had not occurred to Barrett that Ken Arroyo had been supporting anyone but his spoiled son. He tucked the information away to examine at a better time.

Right now, Shelby was making her way to a spot where the tunnel forked into two shafts. One was considerably larger than the other, which was no more than four feet high, the air chilled as a tomb.

"If I'm right," Shelby said, "one of these tunnels will connect with the main shaft on Hatcher's property. That's the one I need to sample to get the best reading."

He looked hard at both. "I don't imagine we're headed into the roomy one, huh?"

She slung her pack on her back and got onto her knees. "In for a penny, in for a pound," she said.

"I never liked that expression," he grumbled.

"Come on, cowboy." She unwrapped a light stick and snapped it to life. The green glow cast an eerie color on the black walls. She set it just outside the entrance. "So your brothers can find us. See? Safety first."

Barrett didn't bother to mention that if the whole place caved in, her little green light was as good as useless.

He hadn't realized until he peered after her into that narrow opening that he might be a touch claustrophobic. Claustrophobia or not, there was no way he was going to stay back and leave Shelby unprotected. On hands and knees, he squeezed his shoulders through the opening.

This had to be the craziest thing he'd done since he was a teenager, all because Shelby Arroyo had got under his skin and into his heart. If he could just get through this wackadoodle adventure and bring her out safely, she would have everything she needed.

He began to squirm his way past the rock that seemed to be trying to smother him. "In for a penny." He sighed.

Shelby wanted to charge ahead but the rocks biting into her palms and kneecaps kept her at a slow pace. That, and the muttered comments from Barrett, who was hard-pressed to stuff his big frame into the narrow tunnel.

Every twenty minutes or so, she activated another light stick to mark the way. The time crept past seven thirty and on to eight o'clock. Though her stomach growled, she ignored it, inching along until a sound brought her up short.

"Barrett? Did you say something?"

"Naw. It's taking all my powers of concentration to crawl along. What did you hear?"

"I thought…" What had it been? A faint gasp of pain? The sound she caught, or imagined, had come from behind them.

Barrett was staring at her, head scrunched under the rock ceiling. "What?"

She shook her head. "Never mind. Just the rock settling or something." She continued on for what seemed like hours until her mouth was parched and her stomach could not be ignored.

"Break time," she announced, her muscles relieved to settle into a sitting position.

Barrett folded himself into an awkward arrangement next to her, accepting the granola bar she provided and guzzling some water from his bottle. "Plan?"

She pulled out her digital thermometer. "The air is getting cooler. It's dropped five degrees in the last five minutes."

"And since Hatcher's tunnel is lower than Oscar's, you figure we're heading in the right direction."

"You're getting good at this," she said, grinning at him. "You could be an assayer."

"Think I'll stick to horses."

A loud thud startled her. "What was that?"

Barrett grabbed his flashlight and scrambled down the tunnel they'd just traversed. Pulse thumping, she scooted behind him. They crawled fifteen feet or so, training their lights into every crevice.

"Nothing," he said. "Some loose rock falling, maybe."

Maybe, she thought. Wasn't that the likeliest explanation? But for a woman who had been shoved in a truck, nearly blown up and almost burned to death, it was easy to jump to other explanations. She didn't want Barrett to see her sinking into paranoia.

"That must have been it," she agreed, and they returned to their spot. Still, the hair on the back of her neck prickled as if stirred by an icy wind. *Don't let Hatcher get inside your thoughts.*

Finishing their snack, they crept onward until the tunnel pinched off completely. She shined her light, sucking in a shocked breath.

"It's blocked."

Barrett stuck his head over her shoulder, his beard giving her shivers.

"Can you switch places with me a minute?"

She flattened herself against the cold rock and he edged forward.

"This is recent," he said grimly. "Someone has rolled a rock across the entrance and filled in around the bottom with debris."

Shelby's nerves twanged. "To what purpose? Was it Hatcher trying to prevent explorers like Charlie?"

"And us?" he offered, not without irony.

She didn't answer. He put a shoulder to the rock and felt it shift. "It's not as heavy as it looks. I can move it."

In a few moments, he'd levered the rock aside and turned to stare at her.

"Shelby, this is getting weird. Someone's been down here. I think we should go back."

"Oh, no," she said. "I may not get another chance.

I'm going to get as far as I can in the next few hours before we need to turn around and meet your brothers."

He sighed. "I thought you'd say that. At least let me go first."

"Okay, I…" She stopped.

"Shelby?"

Her whole body was gripped by an icy blast of fear. "Barrett," she said slowly, shining her light to the rock over his head.

He followed the beam. The light caught a clump of hair clinging to a sharp bit of stone.

"Whose hair?" she whispered. The gloom made it impossible to tell the color. Blond? Black? Brown? Red?

The confusion on his face told her he had no clue either. Whoever it was who had passed this way recently had unintentionally left a calling card. Joe Hatcher, her mind screamed.

The only problem was, Hatcher's hair was snow-white.

The prowler wasn't Hatcher then, Barrett concluded, but that left a million other explanations. Random trespassers who'd done their exploring before Oscar had closed up the mine. Others who enjoyed the fun, breaking in and then boarding up the entrance behind them. Charlie?

The whole thing was giving Barrett a case of the creeps. He didn't suggest turning back, though. The only end to this adventure was through it.

Shelby had pressed on, leaving him to crawl along after her. The tunnel sloped downward and mercifully enlarged, so he could resume a cautious standing position.

The walls, he noticed, were growing damper, trickles of moisture oozing down and muddying the dirt caked on his hiking boots as the passage branched off yet again. He trusted Shelby knew what she was doing, but he could not tell one passage from another except for the glow of the light sticks she was dropping along the way.

She cried out, and he rushed to her. "Look," she said. "Those marks again."

There was indeed another series of red marks, about shoulder high on the wall, speckled with moisture. "They're marking the way to something," she breathed, "I know it."

What kind of weird scavenger hunt was this? Ahead, a scatter of rockfall piled up to the side of the tunnel.

"Odd," Shelby said, shining her light on the ceiling. "Look at the marks. They're scraped and gouged, like someone was using a shovel to bang the rock."

To free the rock detritus that now littered the floor?

She knelt and began pushing away the bigger rocks, rolling them aside. He joined her, a sense of urgency that he did not understand fueling his actions. They'd cleared enough that they were both sweating and had nothing to show for it but sore fingers.

Shelby sat back, shaking her head. "I just don't…"

Barrett held a finger to his lips. "Wait."

They sat in silence for some thirty seconds, listening.

"What do you hear?"

"Air, like a rush of wind from somewhere below us."

Barrett turned on his granddad's flashlight and stuck his face almost to the rock floor where the debris pile had been. One more cluster of rocks remained in the way and he heaved them aside. There in the gap between the tunnel floor and wall was an opening wider than a manhole cover. He eased back to let her see.

"It's too dark. Can I borrow your flashlight?"

He handed it to her, putting a palm on her back to hold her steady as she wriggled her torso into the opening. Her scream cut through his senses.

He grabbed her shoulders and yanked her up. Her eyes were wide with panic, her breath coming in shudders.

"What's wrong?"

She was breathing so rapidly she could not answer.

He took her face in his hands. "Shelby, it's okay. Breathe in and out, real slow."

She tried to comply, but her chest heaved with the effort. He spoke softly to her, soothingly, concentrating on the simple act of breathing. He did not ask again what she'd seen, his only desire to still her panic.

When she calmed down enough that he did not think she would pass out, he took the flashlight from her clutched fingers. The panicked breathing started up again.

"I'm just going to look, that's all. Okay?"

She clamped her lips together and gave him the barest of nods.

He crept to the edge and shone his light down. At first he saw nothing but darkness, the bottom of a subpassage some fifteen feet below. Then the light picked up the gleam of something terrible, unnatural.

Something very, very still.

NINETEEN

Barrett returned to Shelby and sat quietly next to her, his arm around her shoulders, wiping her tears as they fell. Her limbs shuddered with horror, knees drawn up under her chin.

Barrett had seen no more than a twisted body with a shock of hair, the gleam of skin somewhat well preserved due to the cold, no doubt, but subject to decay nonetheless. The dead man lying sprawled against the rocks wore a nylon jacket and sneakers.

"It has to be Charlie," he said. "The hair, it's dark, it must have got caught on the rock back there. He fell in the hole while he was exploring." Even while his mouth constructed impossible scenarios to explain what he'd seen, his brain insisted on coughing up the facts which he knew Shelby was considering, too.

The rock rolled across the entrance. The tunnel debris loosened by some sort of tool to conceal the hole.

"Charlie may have died of natural causes,"

Shelby finally managed, "but someone tried to hide his body."

"Which makes me think it probably wasn't natural causes after all."

Shelby shivered and he gripped her closer. He could hear her struggling to breathe deeply, to drive away the shock of what she'd seen.

She cleared her throat. "The police sent in searchers looking for Charlie but they didn't come this far in, or if they did, they didn't notice the hole in the tunnel floor," she finished.

"We need to get out of here and contact Larraby."

After one more deep breath, she nodded and they got to their feet.

Reluctantly, he settled on his belly, leaning over the hole to take photos of the body with Shelby grimly holding the flashlight and avoiding looking at the grisly mass. Two more light sticks marked the gruesome find to prevent any search-and-recovery personnel from falling into the exposed hole.

They'd done all they could for poor Charlie. Now at least his parents would have closure, the chance to properly mourn their lost son. He pitied them the years they had agonized, not knowing the truth, and the painful years that would stretch on after they did.

Quietly, he said a prayer, feeling the warmth of Shelby's hand joining his. She squeezed his palm and that tiny gesture in the vast darkness lit up a small corner of his heart.

When they were done, he picked up his pack. "We'd better go."

This time she did not argue. When she took a step, she stumbled and grabbed his forearms for support. He folded her close, knowing he shouldn't, understanding there could not be anything between them but feeling an overwhelming urge to comfort her that would not be denied.

"I'm sorry," she whispered, her face pressed to his chest. "My legs aren't working right."

"It's okay. Take your time. We'll go slow and easy on the way back, when you're ready. Not until then."

He wouldn't have minded if she took hours there, leaning on him. It felt so right to be needed by this woman, this flawed, determined, contrary lady from a family he despised. His senses reeled from the shock he'd just experienced and the profound joy of holding her close.

Yep, he was definitely losing what was left of his mind.

She pulled away, wiped her eyes and took in a steadying breath.

"I'm ready. Let's get out of here."

They traversed the way back much slower, the green glow of the light sticks a welcome sight around each corner. When it was time for them to crawl, the distance seemed insurmountable, the cold burrowing into his skin, rocks jabbing his knees and shins.

He decided that he wouldn't care how many tons

of gold lay buried deep in the earth, he'd never go into another mine without a very compelling reason. They got to the place where the tunnel pinched in and the clump of hair clung like some horrible fungus.

Barrett went through the gap first, scraping his shoulders as he did. He was turning around to help Shelby when the sound of a shot fractured the stillness.

Barrett dived instinctively, even though the shot was nowhere near them. He succeeded in bringing Shelby to the floor.

"Gunshots?" she panted.

"Yes," he said. "Near the entrance."

They locked eyes. The entrance where the box of TNT sat innocently in the corner. He did not have time to mouth the words as, a second later, an explosion rang through the caverns, shaking the walls and sending a cascade of debris down upon them.

Shelby screamed and he hauled her close, sheltering them as best he could under a shallow rock projection. All around them the rock seemed to writhe and undulate as if it was a living thing. The tunnel shook so violently he was sure the whole place was going to collapse.

He tucked her head under his torso as the patter of rocks slapped against his back. Thoughts flashed through his mind in a crazy kaleidoscope. He was not afraid to die, he knew a better place awaited, a place where Granddad and Bree were free of pain and suffering. But it occurred to him that he would be leaving behind anger, hatred even, a part of his soul that had not been properly formed into what God intended it to be.

I thought a real man was one who could forgive... like Christ did.

It grieved him that things might end this way. Shelby cried out as a rock bounced off her hip and he tried to pull her closer. She deserved the chance to find her own forgiveness and make peace with her mother. He wanted to holler and shout at the hard stone all around them.

Suddenly, the noise died away and the ground settled itself again. Shelby uncovered her face, breathing hard.

"The shot exploded the dynamite," she panted.

"That would be my theory, too."

"The whole mine might have collapsed. We could have been killed."

There was nothing to be said to that. He watched her expression change from shocked to angry.

"Someone is trying to kill me and it's really starting to get on my nerves." Her voice rose to a shout that bounced off the stone walls, as she swiped the debris from her hair.

He repressed a smile.

"Do you think this is Hatcher's handiwork again?" she demanded.

He didn't want to take the time to dwell on the whodunit. Instead he shook the mess from his hair and beard like a bear emerging from hibernation, and took several cautious steps into the darkness. Turning the corner, he stopped short.

The space was completely filled with shifting rubble that reached fully up to the ceiling. He shoved a hand into it, pushing at the mass, but the rocks pushed right back, pressing him into retreat.

"Guess you got your wish," he said dully, as he returned to her.

She stood with her arms folded, dust coating her hair and clothing. "I'm afraid to ask what that means."

"You wanted to explore the mine and now you're going to have the chance because we're not getting out that way." He jabbed his thumb in the direction of the entrance.

"Completely collapsed?"

"I'm not sure, but in any case it's too filled with debris to pass."

"So we're trapped in here."

"Until we find another exit, yes, or until my brothers and Oscar can shovel us out."

"But...that could take days."

"Months."

She gaped. "Then why do you look so calm about it?"

Because he'd already decided how to play it. It was like working with horses; the calmer you were, the better. "You've mapped this, right? You know it connects to Hatcher's property and we can get out that way."

"That is a theory, mind you, but even if I'm right and we can make our way to Hatcher's entrance safely, his gate is padlocked, remember? And he's supposedly lost the key."

He patted his pack. "I'm prepared this time, but we could also use the escape Emmaline showed us if we can locate it again."

Her eyes narrowed. "Are you being Mr. Cool and Confident because you don't want me to panic?"

He'd told her it might take months to free them, but with the explosion possibly destabilizing the whole mine, there was the chance that it was impossible to clear no matter how much time they had. Considering their limited food and water supplies, the clock was already ticking. Better for her to be searching for a solution than coming to that sobering conclusion.

He pasted on a self-assured smile. "Plenty of people know we're down here. Might as well get out on our own while they're considering what to do." He kept his tone light. "Agreed?"

She searched his face as the seconds ticked by. She was a very smart woman, and he realized he couldn't fool her, not for a minute. She was well aware of the difficulties of moving tons of rock under unstable conditions, but the look on her face said she'd chosen to take a page from his book. Cool and confident beat trembling and terrified any day.

"Yes," she said, tone steady. "But I wasn't going to panic, just for your information."

He admired her for this decision, and for not allowing him to coddle her. Dirty, disheveled as she was, he'd never seen a more beautiful woman. His pulse revved up a notch. *Knock it off, Barrett. Big problems here, or haven't you noticed?* "I didn't figure you would."

"Maybe we can find out more about those red marks while we're poking around down here."

He nodded. "Why not?" he said, squeezing back through the narrow gap. Inwardly, he sighed. God had given them a chance at survival and he would give it everything he had, but it had to be nuts to venture deeper into the mine that had almost killed them.

No, not the mine, he corrected himself. The person who'd shot at the dynamite, who was ready to commit multiple murders to keep them from doing precisely what they were now going to do.

"This is all kinds of crazy," he muttered to himself, thinking she would not hear.

"For sure," came her reply from behind him.

Shelby put on the second jacket she'd packed and checked her supplies. She had twenty or so light sticks left, two bottles of water and several protein bars. How long before they reached Hatcher's end of the mine? If they could find the way.

The light in her headlamp chose that moment to

flicker, reminding her that when the batteries ran out and she'd gone through her refills, they would be in total darkness.

The thought sent a jolt of fear through her. *Plenty of time before that happens*, she silently told herself. *You're not gonna panic, remember?*

More than panic, she felt an overwhelming sense of guilt. Many people had warned her and now, once again, she'd fallen into a disaster, but the worst thing was she'd dragged Barrett right along with her.

His choice, she reminded herself, but the thought rang hollow. Barrett was the sort that would give the shirt off his back for a person in need. Plus, he had that cowboy chivalry thing going that both drove her crazy and made her feel warm and fuzzy.

You're just going to have to get him out of here alive, she told herself sternly.

They reached the spot where the glow sticks marked Charlie's makeshift grave. The path of red marks continued on. She wondered again who'd made the marks. Charlie? Joe Hatcher's wife? Emmaline?

They trudged on for what felt like hours, but her cell phone told her it was only noon. The Thorn brothers would be mounting a rescue effort if they hadn't already been alerted by the explosion.

She had no idea if the entrance collapse had been loud enough to attract attention, or if she and Barrett would be able to receive text messages. Barrett had already tried to send one to his family just in case, and received no reply. The tunnel continued on endlessly until it again branched off.

"Which way?" Barrett said.

The million-dollar question. "I... I don't know." She tested the air temperature of both. "Almost identical."

Barrett played his flashlight over the rock. "Hey, there's one of those red marks."

She joined him. "At least we know someone has been this way before. That's a good sign, right?"

"Yeah." She heard the hesitation in his voice. "Unless it's a trail to lead someone back to Charlie's body."

"For what reason?"

"To make sure they disposed of it properly at some future date, so no one would ever find it."

Like no one would ever find their bodies if they didn't get out of the mine.

"Let's follow it for a while. We can retrace our steps if we need to." She activated a light stick and prepared to move out.

"Lunch break first," Barrett said.

"I don't need a lunch break. I'm not hungry."

"You need water or you'll get dehydrated. Besides, I've got a great snack here." He spread his spare jacket on the ground and patted the spot next to him. She took a seat.

Her mouth fell open as he pulled out a jar of pickles. "You brought pickles with you to go explore a mine?"

"Naw. I brought them to give to Oscar, but I forgot." He popped the lid. "These are the best pickles in California. Believe me, it took me almost a year to master Nanna's recipe."

She accepted a pickle spear and took a bite. Savory with a hint of spice. "You're right," she said with a giggle. "They are good."

He grinned. "I know."

"I never imagined I'd be trapped in a mine with a cowboy, eating homemade pickles."

"Life is a funny thing, isn't it?" They took several swallows of water and capped the bottles, making an unspoken decision to ration their supplies.

Barrett sat up and checked the phone.

She pressed close to see, a flame of hope rising in her.

"Nothing," he said. "Too much interference down here, but it was worth a try."

She finished munching her pickle and checked her own phone. No messages but she noticed the charge was down to 56 percent. "How long will your phone stay charged, Barrett, in case we can somehow send a text when we get closer to the surface?"

"Got the screen turned down and it's running on low power mode. We'll probably be out of here before it dies."

His tone was again Mr. Cool and Confident, but she saw in the twitch of his mouth that he was worried, too.

"I'll power mine off to save the battery." She suppressed the shiver that threatened to march up her spine. How much longer before the phones died?

And how long before their own time ran out?

The muscles in Barrett's shoulders were screaming from being hunched over, but he did not complain. After their lunch break, they'd headed into the tunnel with the marks, but another two hours later, they had encountered no signs that they were headed toward the surface or Hatcher's property.

Making her stop for more water, he pretended to drink deeply, but only took a shallow swig. Still no texts and the charge on his phone continued to drop.

Shelby had fallen silent, trudging along, avoiding the fragments that littered the floor. "So who knew we'd be down here?" she mused aloud.

He understood exactly what she meant because he'd been puzzling over it himself. Who had known they were accessing the mine that morning? "My family, Oscar Livingston and anyone at the inn who might have overheard his conversation with you." He recalled the rustling in the bushes. "If anyone was snooping around Granddad's cabin and heard us talking on the porch."

She shook her head. "It has to be Hatcher. He killed Charlie and doesn't want anyone to discover the body."

"Still doesn't make sense as to why. What reason would he have for killing Charlie in the first place?"

"I don't know."

He sighed. "I'm hungry, time for another pickle break."

He opened the jar and handed her one.

"Thanks."

He took another and fastened the lid back on.

"You're—" His sentence was ripped away, buried in an avalanche of sound as the floor gave way beneath them. He felt himself falling, the jar sailing out of his grasp, and he grabbed at nothing as they plummeted. Shelby tumbled next to him, hair flying, fingers splayed in search of a handhold.

He tried to grab for her but gravity continued to suck him down.

The breath whooshed out of him as he struck the ground. His senses spun, a whirl of pain, confusion and dizziness.

"Shelby," he tried to yell, but his vision narrowed to a tiny pinpoint before darkness overtook him.

TWENTY

The dripping woke him, a ceaseless monotonous tapping that brought him to consciousness. He realized he was on his back on a pile of rubble, both arms thrown wide as if he was making some ridiculous snow angel on the cavern floor. His body screamed with pain and cold. At first he could not tell if his eyes were open or closed in the profound darkness. He tried to sit up, succeeding only in flapping his arms a bit.

"Shelby," he croaked.

There was no answer but the incessant dripping.

Fear, reminiscent of the terror he'd felt at pulling Bree from the wrecked car, invaded every pore in his body. "Shelby," he shouted again, thrashing his legs around to free them from the blanket of rock. His voice echoed back at him, mocking his fear.

He heard a cough and froze. "Shelby?" he said softer. "Are you hurt?" *Please let her answer. Please.*

A flashlight sprang to life and he squinted against

the glare. Rocks crunched against each other and the light swam closer. Still, he tried without success to free himself until he felt a hand on his chest and light blinded him, making him blink.

"Stay still," she said, voice barely louder than a whisper.

"Are you hurt?" he said, unable to see her clearly.

"No, but you are."

"Naw," he started, but she was already moving away. He heard her blow out a breath as she struggled to pull rocks away from his legs. He tried to help, but his limbs behaved as if they were made of rubber.

When she returned, she shined her flashlight around his body, running her hands along his arms and legs, smoothing them over his face, gentler than a spring breeze. He closed his eyes and allowed her touch to push away the pain.

"I don't feel anything broken or out of place, but I only know basic first aid. Did you hit your head on the way down?"

"I hit everything on the way down." He could just make out her faint smile. Score one for the busted-up cowboy. "But I'm okay," he insisted, trying again to sit up with no success. The pain shooting through his side would have made him cry out if he hadn't gritted his teeth.

She gripped his hand. "I think you may have some bruised or broken ribs."

"Yeah," he grunted. "That feels like the right diagnosis." He'd cracked a few ribs getting thrown from horses a time or two. Ribs mended eventually, but he knew full well the injury hurt like gangbusters. He fought back the pain. "Where are we?"

"An underground cavern. It's got a lake and everything."

"Swell. I've been sad that we haven't come across another lake to this point."

"There is some good news."

"By all means, share."

"We're not the first people to hang out down here. Look."

He forced his eyes to focus. In the far side of the cavern sat a couple of wooden barrels, a metal ladder and some old wheels for the ore cars.

"And there's more good news. This was used as some sort of storage area, so that means we have to be getting close to a way out. Miners wouldn't have kept their materials in a place that was completely inaccessible, right?"

"Right," he grated out past the dust in his throat.

She stroked his cheek, her voice soft and comforting. Holding a bottle to his lips, she encouraged him to drink. The liquid was bliss on his tongue.

"In a few minutes, I'll explore our options, but right now, I need to get your other jacket out of your pack. This one is ripped and you have to stay warm to make sure you don't go into shock."

His ears were still ringing but he nodded. "Okay. Where's my pack?"

"You're laying on it. I think it broke your fall. Otherwise you might be dead."

"I'm not totally convinced that I'm actually alive."

She pressed her forehead to his, and spoke nose to nose, her warm breath stirring life back into him. "You're alive, cowboy, because you're groaning. Dead people don't groan."

"Ah. I'll make a note of that." Her lips were so close and he wanted to kiss her. His lips seemed to be the only part of him still working. Certainly his brain had taken a vacation. She pressed a kiss to his cheek and eased away.

After some scrabbling, she managed to pull the pack from underneath him.

"Okay so far?"

"No sweat," he said. At least he had not cried out.

"Can you move your arms and legs at all?"

"'Course." He did an awkward marionette maneuver.

"Nice. If you feel like you can, let me help you sit up on the count of three."

She counted, and with her assistance and a very loud groan, he sat up. The pain flashed bright and hot for a minute before subsiding. Easing on one sleeve at a time, she pulled his jacket over the one he was wearing.

"Are you sure you aren't hurt?" he said. "That was a nasty fall for both of us."

"I was able to hang on for a second before I dropped, but I lost my hard hat. Plus, I fell onto a pile of sand, so that helped. They must have stored sandbags down here at one time." She zipped the jacket to his chin. "Stay put while I check around."

"I can help," he said peevishly. "All my parts work, more or less."

She forced the flashlight into his hand. "You sit here and shine the light around. That's helping."

Grumbling, he complied. His head was still spinning, though he wouldn't admit it to her, but he didn't like being treated like a child. He yanked his phone from his pocket with one hand, biting back an oath. The thing was completely smashed to bits.

"My phone's busted," he griped.

"Mine survived the fall, but still no texting, I just checked. Hey," she cried out, "you won't believe what I just found."

"A walkie-talkie?" he suggested hopefully. "Or a couple of jet packs?"

"No," she said, grin wide as she returned to him. "Better. Your pickles landed in the sand, too. They're not broken!"

He bit off a hearty guffaw when it hurt his ribs too much. "Aside from pickles, what did you find?"

"More good news."

The words were a little too cheerful. "Uh-huh. Let's hear it."

"This cavern is really spectacular actually. Lots of interesting rock formations."

"How about an exit?"

"Oh, there's an exit, all right. It connects to another tunnel and I can see tracks from the ore cars."

"And?"

"And it's the way out onto Hatcher's property, I'm sure of it."

"And?"

"Well, there's a glitch."

He opened the jar and ate a pickle, waiting for the other shoe to drop.

She sighed. "There has been some ground failure so there's about a ten-foot gap between the cavern where we are and the tunnel."

"Ten feet between us and the way out?"

"It appears that way."

He swallowed the pickle and struggled to his feet.

"You should be sitting down," she blurted. "You could pass out."

"Then I guess you should be helping me instead of scolding."

She hooked an arm under his shoulder and he stood, woozy at first, but relieved to find that he did not notice any new areas of pain. Together they staggered over to the cavern's edge.

"Careful," she said as he peered below. The view was obscured by darkness. Only when she shined the flashlight across could he see the tunnel ahead, the edge of the rails twisting off where the ground had collapsed underneath them. She was right, the distance was a good ten feet.

He stared down into the abyss. "How far down does it go?"

"I'm not sure."

Painfully, he bent to pick up a rock and tossed it over the edge. Time stretched out endlessly until finally he heard a splash, seemingly fathoms away, as the rock connected with some hidden lake.

His gaze fastened on hers.

"So all we need to do is figure out a way across," she said.

"Yep, that's all there is to it." He let out a deep sigh. "Right."

Shelby wished she could light a fire to keep them warm, but there was not enough flammable material to fuel it, and it was a risky idea anyway with all the trapped gases she might ignite with a mere spark. Instead she sat side by side with Barrett, shivering, sharing a protein bar to quiet their aching stomachs.

She was deeply grateful that he had not suffered any worse damage, but she worried that he might slip into shock, or that he could have internal injuries. Their options were narrowing with every passing moment, along with their supplies. They were down to less than two bottles of water since Barrett's had both been smashed on impact. Her mouth was already parched. She allowed herself a swallow of water and insisted Barrett drink one, too, in spite of his protests.

His phone was crushed and hers low on charge,

so she powered it down after she checked the time. It was almost four o'clock in the afternoon. Had the Thorn brothers started trying to dig them out via Oscar's entrance? Or might they have decided the best way was to go through Hatcher's property? It grieved her to think how Barrett's brothers and parents must be frantic with worry, Oscar, too.

But you had to go through with it, didn't you? she chided herself. No matter that it put Barrett's life at risk or flew in the face of good sense. She deserved the consequences of her bullheaded determination, but Barrett and his family did not.

Anger at her helplessness bubbled up. *But people don't always get what they deserve, now do they?* she thought.

Bree hadn't. Her own mother hadn't. Right then in the crippling darkness, she remembered her mother's soft touch, always smelling of scented lotion. She missed it desperately, craving the chance to hold her mother's hand again.

The memory doused the anger and lit her with a new determination. She and Barrett would get out of this and she would go to see her mother. Period.

Enough with the sentimentality. Figure out an escape plan, she commanded herself.

She played through the scenarios in her mind. There was only one way out and that was to get across to the tunnel. Could she leap across the chasm? Even running at full speed, she doubted she could make the jump, especially in her weakened and hungry state. Barrett most certainly could not. So how were they going to cross the gap?

The only workable idea she could think of was the long metal ladder left to rust for who knew how long in the forgotten cavern. She got up and examined it. It had to be at least fifteen feet, made of heavy iron, built to last. Pressing a foot to the rungs, she figured the metal was as sound as it needed to be. It only had to support her weight long enough for her to get across. Then she would summon help somehow. She'd just have to pray that she could get a text out or scream loud enough that someone would cut through the lock on Hatcher's gate, if that was indeed where she wound up.

If…if…if.

Barrett joined her. "No way," he said, as if reading her thoughts.

"I'm just testing out an idea."

"Well, quit it 'cause it's a very bad idea."

"I didn't ask for your opinion."

"I'm providing it free of charge."

She ignored him, dragging the ladder over to the edge of the crevasse. He followed, issuing a steady stream of discouragement, which she disregarded. "Can you put weight on this end and keep it from angling downward? I'm going to slide it out and see if it will reach the other side."

"This is a…"

"Bad idea, I know," she said, straining all her muscles to slide the ladder out into the darkness.

Inch by inch she pushed it forward, Barrett weighing the other end down to keep it horizontal. He grunted with pain but he did not slow his efforts. Sweat dripped down her face as the metal grated against the rock on the other side.

"It worked," she said, wiping her hands on her jeans. One end of the ladder rested on the lip of the tunnel, the other on the sandy floor of the cavern. Hope flickered to life.

Barrett watched her, arms folded. "So you think that ladder is stable enough to support a human body?"

"Yes," she said with certainty.

"And you figure the tunnel edge isn't going to give way as soon as we put any more weight on it?"

"Pretty sure, yes." Was she? There was no way to be certain that the lip of rock would hold. A lump formed in her throat and she longed for a deep drink of ice-cold water. Seconds ticked by accompanied by an incessant dripping from somewhere in the cavern, mocking her thirst.

He finally shook his head. "Shelby Arroyo, there is no way on this planet I am letting you crawl across that ladder."

Her chin went up. "You can't stop me."

"Yes, I can."

He stepped forward, towering over her. She feared he was going to put her over his shoulder, injured ribs or no injured ribs. Instead, he stepped around her, blocking her from the ladder.

"What are you doing?"

He rolled up the sleeves of his jacket. "I'm going to cross and then I'll get help."

She tried to edge in front of him, but he moved her aside. "You're in no condition to do this, Barrett."

"The only condition a person needs to be in to do this is to be out of his mind, and I reckon I fit the bill."

"Barrett, no." She grabbed his arm. "You're heavier than I am, you're injured. I got you into this mess. I should go."

"I walked into the mess of my own accord. Eyes wide open."

"No. This is my fault and I am going to get us out of this."

He took hold of her hands and held them to his chest. Though the darkness dulled the hue, she imagined the intense blue of his gaze riveted on her face.

"Shelby, I cannot watch you risk your life. I am going to cross first because it's the right thing to do."

Tears gathered in her eyes and she whacked a palm against his chest, making him wince. "That makes no sense, it's just dumb cowboy chivalry."

"Maybe, but it doesn't change my decision."

"I can't let you do this." Her voice shook. "You've been in trouble since the moment we met."

"That is true," he said, something wistful in his voice.

"And I don't want you to sacrifice yourself for me, do you hear me, Barrett Thorn?" The tears trickled down and he put his mouth to her forehead. She held him close, fiercely, ignoring the pain it might cause him, trying to squeeze some sense into him.

"My dumb cowboy chivalry says a man needs to do what he can in this world," he murmured in her ear. "I've disappointed you and myself. I can't be the kind of man you deserve, but I can do this and I'm gonna."

"I won't let you."

"It's not your decision to make." He pulled away, kissed her on the temple and then on the cheek. She found her head tipping up to meet his mouth and for a split second it felt as if her heart reached out and joined with his.

Sparks tripped across her senses, and she grasped the nape of his neck, holding him close, kissing him. He released her and trailed a hand through her hair. Desperately, she tried to think of something that would change his mind.

Bending, he picked up his hard hat and put it on her head. "It's going to be okay."

But what if it wasn't? What if he fell? What if…?

Before she could rally another argument, he got on his knees and crept out onto the first few rungs of the ladder. The metal creaked, twanging her nerves. Time ground to a halt and even her shallow breaths seemed loud to her frazzled senses. Two more rungs out and he was well away from the side, perched on the rickety ladder, hovering over a drop that would certainly kill him.

She could make out the white gleam of his hands, a flicker of his cheek, ashen in the darkness. Twisting her hands together, she realized they had not prayed together before he put his life on the line.

"Lord God," she breathed. Another creak of the ladder made her stop, pulse slamming in her throat.

Light. He needed more light than the glow from her headlamp and the flashlight. With clumsy fingers, she pulled out a glow stick from her backpack. "Barrett, I'm going to throw a light stick over to the far side to help you see, okay?"

"Fire away," he said.

She activated the chemicals and launched the stick across the chasm. It arced through the black, a whirling pinwheel of green, landing on the lip of the rock.

"Good shot," he called. "I can see where I'm going now."

Inch by painful inch, he crept forward. Each movement had to be tugging on his ribs, but he made no complaint. She kept the flashlight trained as best she could to make out his progress and help light his way. Only three feet to go as he inched closer to the luminescent green marker. She blew out a breath to relieve the excruciating tension.

With a smack of flesh on iron, his right hand

slipped off the rung and he fell heavily against the ladder, grunting as his torso impacted the metal. She screamed, body stiff with terror. He clung there for a minute. It hurt to breathe, her every muscle taut as steel wire as the seconds ticked by.

Barrett, please don't fall. Please...

With excruciating slowness, he got into a crawling position again.

Finally able to draw breath, she felt like laughing and crying all at the same time.

You're going to make it, Barrett.

He had only a few feet to go now. The insane plan was actually working. Barrett was gradually creeping across to safety. She realized her hands were balled into fists and she forced her fingers to relax.

Wishing she'd thought to urge him to carry his pack with some food and water, she considered his next steps. The tracks would take him to the surface. They had to, or at least close enough that he could yell for help. Her lungs began to return to a seminormal rhythm as he eased along the rusted iron rungs.

She could practically hear him now saying, "That was all kinds of crazy."

It would be a story to tell his family, for sure.

The smile died on her face as the ladder snapped in two with a shriek of metal.

TWENTY-ONE

Barrett felt the ladder give way underneath him. He clung to the metal with all the strength he could muster, his knees and elbows scraping against the rock wall as the ladder ricocheted off the rocks, plummeting downward. The spiraling movement and the rain of debris dizzied his senses.

He managed to hook an arm over the end of the twisted rail that jutted out over the chasm. The sudden stop in momentum jarred every nerve into an avalanche of pain. Hanging there by one arm, the pieces of the ladder fell away beneath him until they made a distant splash as they plunged into the water far below. Shelby's screams ricocheted off the cavern walls.

He knew he could not hold on for long. His ribs sent ribbons of fire through his body as he wriggled to get his other arm around the rail. The metal was cold and damp, like something long dead, but at the moment it was his best friend. Hanging there cost him every bit of effort but it was not enough.

His only hope was to hook a leg up over the rail, which would give him enough leverage to shimmy his way out of the chasm. Muscles tensed to the breaking point, he tried to heave his leg over, but he could not manage it. Panting, he allowed himself to rest a moment.

"Barrett," Shelby screamed again into the darkness. She appeared to be lying on her stomach staring down. Her voice was brittle as glass, edged with hysteria.

"I'm okay," he shouted up, but he was not sure it was enough to carry back to her. Knowing she was up there, frantic, perhaps thinking him dead, fueled him to try again and he swung his leg up a second time, managing to curl just the heel of his boot over the edge of the beam. He'd done it, but he was too depleted to do anything more. His muscles were hard-pressed even to hold him there, growing weaker by the moment.

"Move, move," he ordered his aching limbs, but he did not have the strength.

The weight of his failure pressed in on him. If he did not succeed, who knew how long it would be before help arrived for Shelby.

Arms trembling, he focused on breathing, despair permeating his bones like the relentless cold. *Shelby*, he wanted to call out, *this isn't your fault*. His sweaty palms began to lose their grip on the clammy metal.

"Lord, save her," he breathed. "Don't let her die here alone."

Seconds ticked into minutes. He became aware of shouting from somewhere above him, low voices, deep and masculine. His mind wanted to consider that strange fact but he could not bring his mental powers into focus.

Something thudded against his shoulder and still he clung, sweat rolling down his face.

"Barrett."

Then Jack was somehow next to him, tethered to a rope.

"How…?"

"Not important. Hold on." Jack wrapped a rope around his middle and grabbed him up in an enormous bear hug. "Ready," he shouted.

From somewhere above, the rope was hauled up, cinching around his middle and squeezing until he thought he would pass out from the pain.

"Shelby," he murmured. "You've got to get her out."

"One rescue at a time," Jack said. Moments later, they were lifted out into the tunnel by Owen and his father. Oscar was right behind him, standing ready with a sturdy twenty-foot aluminum ladder.

His father gripped Barrett's arm after Jack lowered him onto the floor. "That was not a sight I ever want to see again."

"Me neither, sir. How are we going to get her out?"

"Keegan is setting that up right now," Jack said.

Keegan. Good. If there was anyone skilled at cheating death, it was his youngest brother. Once Barrett quieted his breathing, he could hear Keegan, along with Owen, shouting directions across the gorge to Shelby. He watched as Owen and Keegan used the same procedure he and Shelby had with their sturdy ladder, easing it out across the chasm, a rope looped through one of the rungs.

"Tie the rope around your waist," Keegan shouted to Shelby.

"Her hands are numb with cold. The ground is unstable," Barrett said. "The rope might not be enough. I need to cross over to her."

They ignored him.

"Hey," he said, earning a look from Keegan, "this isn't safe."

Keegan cocked his head. "Considering Oscar's entrance is covered under three tons of rock, this is the only option. Besides," he said with a grin, "I've done stuff like this plenty of times. It'll be fun and she'll have a great story to tell afterward."

Barrett opened his mouth to retort, but his father stopped him. "There is a rescue crew on its way, but I think we are her best chance just now."

Barrett tried to breathe his way to some sense of calm. "How did you find us?"

"Heard the explosion. Couldn't get through the rockfall so we let ourselves onto Hatcher's property."

"He allowed you into the mine?"

His father shook his head. "He wasn't home so we let ourselves in."

"You trespassed?"

He shrugged, a mischievous twist to his mouth. "Not going to let my boy and his girl die, am I?"

She's not my girl, he wanted to say, but right then the group grew silent as Keegan and Owen steadied the ladder. Barrett struggled to his feet.

"Stay put," Jack said.

"I need to be there," he hissed through gritted teeth. His brothers had brought lanterns that illuminated the chasm much better than their meager flashlights. Vast, silent and unforgiving, the tomb of stone had been left undisturbed for years. He paid attention only to the small figure on hands and knees, making her way across the sturdy aluminum slats.

"That's it," Keegan said. Owen, Jack and his father had all taken hold of the other end of Shelby's safety rope, legs braced in case she fell. Barrett's stomach was a tight knot.

Her face, ashen and scrunched in concentration, swam closer and closer. He could hardly hold himself back from scrambling across that ladder to retrieve her. Metal creaking, an icy wind blowing through the pitch-black, he gritted his teeth and waited.

"You got this," Keegan said. "Piece of cake."

Another five seconds of agony and she was across. When she was safely past the rock lip, Barrett could not wait any longer, grabbing her up in a hug that sent pain through his side.

She was shivering, breathing shallow. Jack wrapped a blanket around her back. Owen pressed a water bottle into her hand but she was shaking so badly she could not open it.

Barrett uncapped the bottle for her and held it to her lips while she drank. With a sudden roar, the ground trembled under them as the lip of rock gave way and the ladder spiraled into the depths.

Keegan let out a low whistle. "Gonna have to get ourselves a new ladder."

Barrett laughed and held Shelby close.

Shelby did her best to keep up with the Thorn family and Barrett as they crept through the tunnel. If she showed the slightest signs of faltering, they would pick her up, and she could not allow that.

They'd moved a safe distance away from the collapsing rock and given her time to get her body working again, but her limbs still shook as they walked back to Hatcher's property. It was a small comfort to know that she had been right; the passages did connect.

She stopped, fished a bag out of her back pocket and collected a sample of rock, stowing it in her backpack along with the other.

Jack and Owen looked on in astonishment.

"Still on the job?" Owen asked. Even in the dim light, she could read the distrust on his face. She couldn't exactly blame him. Her bullheaded dedication to her job had almost cost their brother's life. Instead of answering, she pushed ahead, filled with a burning desire to get out of the rocky tomb.

When they finally exited the mine into the moonlit night, she thought she'd never experienced air so pure and precious. Barrett must have felt the same, too. He stood with his face tipped toward the sky, pulling in deep breaths, one hand pressed to his side. Evie Thorn greeted them, squeezing them both into a joyous embrace, her face stark with emotion.

Hatcher was there, too, arms crossed, glowering, Emmaline peeping over his shoulder. "Cut through my lock," he grumbled. "Destroyed my property."

"And as I told you, we will reimburse you in full for the replacement of that lock," Evie said. "And you won't raise a fuss, because if it was your daughter in the same predicament, you would have trespassed on our property without a second thought, wouldn't you?"

He looked at his boots.

"Wouldn't you?" she repeated.

His mouth twisted. "Yeah, I'd do most anything for Emmaline."

Shelby was astonished with Evie Thorn's powers of persuasion as the woman turned her attention to Barrett. "You're going to the clinic," she told her son.

"Yes, ma'am." Shelby thought he must be in significant discomfort to have agreed without a word of argument.

"You, too," she said to Shelby.

"I'm not hurt."

"Your jacket sleeve is torn and I can see blood through the tear. You're both dehydrated at the very least. We'll let the doctors clean you up." With that, she marched to the truck and opened the passenger door, waiting while Shelby meekly shouldered her pack. She passed Barrett on the way.

"Don't worry," he whispered. "Even Keegan does what Mama says when she takes that tone."

"I heard that, Barrett," Evie said. "It's a twenty-minute drive to the clinic and you're both shivering, so quit talking and get into your brother's truck."

"Yes, ma'am," he said.

Shelby slid into the front seat of the other vehicle between Tom and Evie. When the heater fired up to high, she felt the delicious warmth bringing her limbs back to life and every scrape and bruise made itself known with a throb. Evie made sure Shelby's lap was draped with another blanket. Then she sat, hands clasped in her lap while Shelby told her about the body they'd found. Tom's forehead creased as he listened. Evie gasped.

"Was it that poor boy who stayed at Oscar's inn?"

"I think so. He might have died accidentally, but someone tried to hide his body."

Evie stared at her. "Shelby," she said quietly, "this has got to stop. Whatever is going on with this mine has created too many close shaves. You were both almost killed today. Please tell me you're not going back into that mine. Not again."

"I don't have any plans to." She wanted to stop there, but she owed these good people the truth. "Unless I need another sample."

"No," Evie repeated firmly. "That's not good enough. I want to hear you say you won't go back down there, not with my son."

"Evie…" Tom started.

"I can't stay quiet." Her eyes searched Shelby's. "Barrett is obviously fond of you and so are we. He feels a duty to protect you, a commitment that I haven't seen in him since Bree was alive, but he's already lost one woman he loved and I don't want that to happen to him again."

"I don't want him to risk himself for me. I didn't ask him to."

Her eyes flashed. "Don't you see that you didn't have to? I think he's falling in love with you, and that means nothing would ever prevent him from standing by your side."

Falling in love with her? "You're wrong," she wanted to reply, but Evie had taken Shelby's hand.

"Say you'll walk away from the mine and never go back."

A pang of regret stabbed her heart. Evie was right. Any mother would insist on the same thing, but she could not make a promise to Evie Thorn that would mean she had to break the one to her uncle.

"I still haven't completed my work for Uncle Ken. I can't make a promise like that."

Evie chewed her lip. When she finally spoke, her voice was a ragged whisper. "Then promise me you'll stay away from my son."

Tom cleared his throat. "We don't have the right to interfere, Evie."

"Yes, we do," she said, tears sparkling on her lashes. "After what he's endured, I can't stand by and watch another disaster in the making. He's finally begun to heal."

Tom sighed. "Let's talk about this later when we've got our nerves under control."

Evie nodded, mouth tight, and stared out the window.

Shelby kept her own gaze front and center, willing herself not to cry. *Stay away from my son...* How could they not understand her desire to protect her uncle? Did it really come down to betraying him in order to follow her burgeoning feelings for Barrett? She recalled the absolute terror she'd felt when the ladder had collapsed, throwing him into the abyss. Did she care for him enough to walk away from her uncle?

Is that what love meant? Turning your back on your family?

No, she told herself. She'd turned her back on her mother, busied herself with school and her career, allowing anger and resentment to cement the wall between them. Whatever she felt for Barrett was not strong enough to drive her to abandon Uncle Ken.

Besides, Barrett had said he could not give her what she deserved, so deep were his own feelings of resentment. Thoughts whirled through her mind along with a cascade of hurts and hopes. She could not be with Barrett unless she gave up on Uncle Ken, and Barrett was not able to give his heart to her because of his endless rage at that same man.

Oh, Lord, she pleaded silently, *what should I do?*

There was no answer in her soul, no comfort as the miles unrolled before them.

TWENTY-TWO

After Barrett was thoroughly poked, prodded, hydrated and had his ribs taped, he found Officer Larraby waiting. He'd refused any pain medicine other than a couple of aspirin and fatigue was not helping him concentrate on the questions. Nor was the detached look on Shelby's face. Was she experiencing delayed shock? He didn't blame her. As the hours after their escape ticked by, the magnitude of the whole trauma was starting to sink in.

They sat in an empty waiting room with Larraby and another officer while his parents and brothers clustered nearby.

Barrett explained again about the body and did his best to describe the location. "I took pictures…" His voice trailed off. "But we used my phone," he said, "and it was smashed in the fall."

"We might still be able to lift something from it." Larraby held out a palm.

Barrett felt his cheeks warm. "I left it in the cavern."

"I don't suppose you picked it up?" Larraby cast a peeved glance at Shelby.

She shook her head. "No, but I can confirm everything he said. You should be able to find the spot where the body is buried and maybe the place where we found the hair."

"Oh, you think so, do you? Not until we get some engineers to shore up the place and a backhoe to remove a ton of rubble. Oscar's given us carte blanche to do whatever we need to, but we'll still have to bring in people from outside the county to make this happen and that costs time and money."

"Do it, then," Barrett said irritably. "The family needs their son's remains. It's only right."

"Your family is fortunate we aren't digging out *your* remains," he said, glaring at Barrett, before he cast a glance at Shelby. "Or yours. We contacted your uncle on his cell phone and he's half-frantic. He's on his way home right now."

Shelby looked at the floor. "I didn't mean for any of this to happen."

"Well, that makes it all better now, doesn't it?" Larraby said.

"Hey," Barrett snapped, "no harm done and we discovered a possible murder. You should be thanking us."

"That'll be the day."

"The red marks," Shelby said suddenly. "Someone left them as a set of directions. Maybe it was the murderer, who intended to come back and re-move the body at some point."

Larraby held up a palm. "First off, we don't know this was murder. Second, red marks could have been left by anyone. We'll investigate, but for now, stay out of the mine."

"I concur," Barrett's mother said. He saw an odd look on her face as she gazed at Shelby and he won-dered what the two of them had talked about on the way to the clinic.

All he could think about was how petrified he'd been watching Shelby crawl across that ladder. He wanted to touch her, to hold her, to reassure him-self that she really was there and not lying broken at the bottom of the chasm. He itched for the oth-ers to move away and give him a moment alone with Shelby.

She straightened and checked her phone. "It's a text from my uncle. He's on his way home from the airport."

Barrett's heart sank. He'd not realized until that moment how much he liked having her on the ranch.

"I have to go," she said.

"We'll drive you," Barrett said, giving his broth-ers a look.

Jack nodded. "Sure. We can stop at the ranch first and get your things if you'd like."

"No, thank you," she said. "I will find my own way home."

Barrett started to object but she simply walked

out of the waiting room. His mother tried to put a restraining arm on his shoulder but he got painfully to his feet and followed. "Shelby, wait."

When she did not slow, he tried to hurry but his legs felt battered and scraped. "Shelby." She did not pause until he touched her arm. Finally, she turned.

"What is it, Barrett?" Her eyes looked pained and he wondered if she'd been hurt more seriously than she let on.

He felt suddenly tongue-tied. "Well, I mean, I don't think you should be leaving alone."

"Why not?"

"Um, I… I'm worried about you."

She caught her lip between her teeth and he could see moisture glittering in her eyes. "Barrett, I am sorry I got you into more trouble, but it won't happen again. I appreciate all you've done for me, I really do, but it's best if we go our separate ways."

"Separate ways?" he repeated dumbly.

"Yes. I'm going back home to my uncle and you're going with your family. That's the way it should be."

Of course she was right. His life had been simpler, easier without her, but the words stung like wasps. "Did I…did I say something wrong back there in the mine?"

She tilted her head and he wanted to reach out and push the strands of hair from her forehead, but he stood frozen.

"No, not at all. You've been so good to me and

gone way out on a limb to help me, and so has your family, but my first loyalty has to be to my uncle and your family expects your loyalty to be to them."

"My loyalty is not in question."

"It will be, and so will your safety if you hang around with me. Please take good care of yourself, okay?"

"Shelby," he started.

She moved quickly, pressing a kiss on his cheek, and left through the sliding exit doors.

He felt a presence behind him and turned to find his mother. "I begged her not to go into that mine anymore, and she could not promise that she wouldn't, so…"

"So?"

"So I asked her not to be involved with you."

For a second, anger licked hot inside his gut. "Mama…"

"I know it wasn't my place, but I was scared. She said her first duty was to her uncle."

He let out a gush of air. Ken Arroyo…the root of all the heartbreaks in Barrett's life. If things had been different, he mused, if Shelby wasn't the man's niece…but she was, and all that Shelby and Barrett had gone through was for the purpose of helping him out, the man who'd raised a feckless son, the boy who killed Barrett's wife.

He looked at his mother, pain that began when Bree died etched deeply in the crow's-feet around her eyes. He realized how he must have reawakened that pain by his dangerous interactions with Shelby. He could not be mad at her.

"If you…if you want her to be a part of your life," she said, "I will apologize to her, Barrett. I'll drive over there right now."

My first loyalty has to be to my uncle.

His mother was right. He folded her in his arms and kissed the top of her head. "I love you, Mama."

She sighed softly against his chest. "Can we go home now, honey?"

"Yes, ma'am," he said. "Let's do that."

Shelby could hardly keep her eyes open when she arrived by taxi back at the Arroyo Ranch late that night. Her uncle met her with both anger and rejoicing.

"You never should have gone. What were you thinking?" Then he clutched her in a bear hug that nearly squeezed the air out of her.

She endured his relentless questions. "The bottom line is that I got the samples."

That stopped him short. "You did?"

She nodded. "I've arranged with an assayer in Copperopolis to analyze them tomorrow at his lab."

His eyes widened. "I would never have wanted you to risk your life, but I am glad to know something good came out of it."

"Maybe. We'll know after I complete the analysis."

"Well, I'm going with you, of course."

"It's a date," she said, smiling. "Ten o'clock."

"And I'm contacting the Thorns to have my horses returned ASAP."

She frowned. "They were very gracious to take them."

He lifted a shoulder. "Yes," he admitted. "I suppose they were. I'll be sure to thank them."

After the hottest, longest shower she could manage, she pulled on some blissfully clean clothing. Her body felt less achy in spite of the gouge on her arm, but the throb in her chest had not dissipated since she left the clinic. The look on Barrett's face had almost broken her will to leave.

But he'd made it clear, hadn't he, before the cave-in? There could be no future for them anyway. His mother had only confirmed that. The Thorns were good people and Shelby would not threaten their future simply to chase after her own fleeting happiness with a man who did not want her enough.

Fatigue overwhelmed her and she lay down on the bed, pulling the covers up to her chin. As she drifted off to sleep, she thought of the Thorn family room, the smell of Evie's cooking, the good-natured ribbing of the brothers and the sad blue eyes of one particular brother.

Shelby decided that a dose of sunshine might help lift the gloom the next morning. The December frost had long since melted away, leaving the ground damp. She'd just crested the slope moving toward the stables when she caught sight of the Thorns' horse trailer parked near the pasture.

. She froze. "Oh, quit it, you ninny. After the horses are delivered, you won't see any more of Barrett." Besides, she thought, it was likely Barrett wasn't even participating in the process with his banged-up ribs and the way they'd ended things at the clinic.

Standing tall and pushing her hair behind her ears, she marched toward the pasture, face flushing when she realized Barrett was indeed there, coaxing Diamond from the trailer. Pattycake and Buddy were already freed, close together and happy in the pasture.

Emmaline was also there, to Shelby's surprise, elbows propped on the pasture fence watching Barrett. Shelby joined her.

"Are you okay?" Emmaline asked.

"Yes, a little worse for wear, but not bad."

Emmaline cocked her head. "It's like you are invincible or something."

Shelby laughed. "Not anywhere close."

Emmaline quirked a grin. "I hope it's okay that I came. You said…" She shoved her hands in the pockets of her jeans. "You said I could come and see Diamond anytime."

"And I meant it."

They watched Barrett ease the nervous horse from the trailer before he led Diamond to the pasture and let her loose, shutting the gate behind. After a moment's hesitation, he joined them.

Emmaline moved away a few paces, pulling an apple from her pocket, face shining.

"Here, Diamond. Remember me? Come here, girl."

Barrett kept his gaze on the horse.

"Thank you for taking care of them," Shelby said.

"Your uncle already thanked us and offered to pay."

"Which you didn't accept."

"Correct." Now he glanced at her. "They weren't any trouble. Are you…okay?"

She nodded. "Scraped is all. You?"

He shrugged in typical fashion. "No lasting damage. Did you, uh, get your samples safely home?"

She nodded. "Taking them to a lab in Copperopolis at ten to analyze."

Emmaline stretched her arm farther over the fence. "Diamond," she crooned softly. "You used to be mine, remember? Red apples were your favorite and I brought you one every day."

The horse sniffed the air, nostrils flared.

"That's it," Emmaline said. "You remember now."

The horse suddenly wheeled around and raced away, legs flying swiftly over the green grass. Emmaline sagged, the apple falling from her fingers. "She doesn't know me anymore."

"It may take some time," Shelby said, "but she will learn to trust you again."

"That's what my father used to say about my mother. 'It will take some time, but she will grow to love it here in Gold Bar.'" Emmaline's features hardened. "Do you see any sign of her coming back?"

Shelby pitied the girl. Abandoned by her mother, with an angry man like Joe Hatcher for a father. Where was the tenderness in this girl's life? "I'm sorry, but please don't give up on Diamond."

"Too late," Emmaline said. "She's got you now."

"Emmaline…" Shelby started, but the girl had already trudged away.

"She's had a hard life," Barrett said.

"I'll find her later and encourage her to try again with Diamond."

He nodded. "So, uh, I guess I'd better be going."

She tried for levity. "Horses waiting for your attention?"

He huffed out a breath, rubbing a hand across his close-cut beard. "I've been banned from most duties until my ribs heal. I had to throw a fit to get to bring the horses over here. Now I'm relegated to building tables for the Christmas Eve dinner."

"I hope it's a great event," she said.

"I wish…" he started. "Nothing. I've gotta go. I picked up a new phone, same number, you know, if you need anything. Hope your samples turn out the way you want."

Nothing has turned out the way I want, she thought, watching him climb back in the trailer and drive away.

TWENTY-THREE

Shelby carried the samples to the truck and her uncle climbed behind the wheel. "Ready to find out once and for all?"

"Yes," she said. "More than ready."

As they clattered over the drive, she gripped the samples tight. She and Barrett had almost died for this small bag of rocks. Her mind wandered, thinking of his laughter in the cavern, the taste of pickles trickling across her memory.

"That went better than I expected," her uncle was saying.

"Oh, I'm sorry. What did you say?"

He smiled at her as he took the turn onto a quiet stretch of highway that curved away through the wooded foothills. "My business trip. I have someone who offered full price for my property. I hate to let go of the land, but it will ease the pressure for a while anyway, maybe until Devon is released."

"Next year?"

"Or sooner, maybe." He shifted in his seat and

cleared his throat. "Devon told me that Barrett Thorn sent him a letter."

She started. "Really?"

"Said Barrett made it clear he forgave Devon, that he was praying for him."

Shelby swallowed a lump in her throat. "That's wonderful."

Uncle Ken's lips twisted in thought. "Yeah. I don't know how I feel about it. Devon's life is ruined and it's not like Barrett's forgiveness is going to make one bit of difference."

It will make all the difference, she thought.

"And who is Barrett to be offering prayers for my son, like he's some kind of perfect man himself?"

Who was Barrett? A man learning to forgive. Something warm and soft washed over her heart. She hoped his actions would give him and his family peace.

Uncle Ken opened his mouth to talk when his glance went to the rearview mirror.

"What in the world…?"

Shelby jerked around to see a battered pickup bearing down on them. The glare made it impossible to see the driver, but clearly the driver saw them, pushing the truck forward, closing the gap between them.

"He's going to hit us," Shelby screamed.

Uncle Ken jammed his foot to the gas pedal. "Hold on," he shouted. Their truck was bigger, which made it more ungainly, so their pursuer had the advantage. At first it looked as though they would be able to outpace the smaller truck.

"Look out," Shelby cried. "Sharp turn."

Ken cranked the wheel hard and tried to slow enough to safely navigate the tight bend in the road.

With a crash of metal, the truck behind them plowed into their fender.

Shelby was jerked hard, hitting her shoulder on the door frame. Uncle Ken fought the wheel but the impact slammed their vehicle and it skidded sideways off the road.

Time slowed as the truck began to tip over, twisting and turning as it plunged down the hillside. Dark tree trunks flickered in a dizzying parade by the windshield. There was a crack, and the windshield shattered. Bits of metal and glass flew around her face. Finally, with a massive bang, the truck crashed headfirst into the twisted trunk of an oak tree. The impact jarred them both violently.

For several moments, Shelby was unable to do anything but breathe. The truck had righted itself, but the front end was mashed against the tree trunk. She forced herself to look sideways. Uncle Ken was slumped against the driver's door, eyes closed.

"Uncle Ken," she said, trying to reach him, but her seat belt was jammed. She heard the distant sound of a car door slamming up on the road. Was it help? Or the person who had just tried to kill them? With frantic fingers, she yanked at the seat belt but it would not give.

Phone.

She wriggled and thrashed until she could free the pocket of her jacket from under the belt. She texted Barrett.

Help. Accident.

She added the last route marker they'd passed.

Now there were footsteps approaching their truck, warily, stealthily. Not a passerby, come to rescue them. A killer, come to finish the job. Her skin crawled.

She again pressed the seat belt button and this time it gave way. She grabbed her bag of samples. If someone was ready to kill for the rocks, they might be her only bargaining chip to keep her and her uncle alive.

The door was stuck, so she kicked aside the broken glass and climbed out, fighting dizziness. Listening hard, she heard the footsteps off to her right, behind a screen of prickly shrubs. Head down, she raced over the grass, looping around to circle back to the road where she had a better hope of flagging down help.

Fear for Uncle Ken made it hard to move. Was he dead? Bleeding out? Was she leaving him behind to die?

Just run, get help. Fighting dizziness, she scurried behind a pile of rocks and stopped to get her bearings. Shadows loomed all around her but she poked her head above the rocks, identifying a relatively clear route leading up to the road. Unfortunately, it was exposed.

Stay put and hide?

Run for help?

The agony of indecision nearly overcame her. One thought pounded repeatedly through her mind. *Run.*

She counted to three, hugged her sample bag tight and sprinted.

Adrenaline fired her muscles. She covered several yards before she heard the footsteps pursuing her. Stumbling over fallen branches, panting, she pushed on until a hand grabbed her hair, yanking her back and sending her sprawling. She tried to scramble away, but the arms that turned her over were strong, one forearm pressed hard on her throat.

She looked up into the hard face of Joe Hatcher. He ripped the samples out of her grasp.

"Listen," he said, "I didn't want it to be this way. None of this would have happened if you could have kept your nose out of my mine."

"What is down there?" she breathed. "What are you so scared for me to find? Did you kill Charlie? Is that it?"

He pulled her hair until she stopped talking. "Just give up, you wretched troublemaker. Why won't you get out of Gold Bar and never come back? When I pushed you in the trunk I was sure that would scare you off for good."

She blinked back tears of pain. "Give me back my samples."

"I told you," he said, breath hot on her face, "you have to get out of town or…"

"Or you'll kill me like you've been trying to do since I got here?"

"I didn't want to hurt you," he hissed. "You just wouldn't let it go." He pulled a knife from his pocket, the blade glittering.

Shelby writhed and tried to scream but he clapped a hand over her mouth.

"Remember that I didn't want to," he said, lifting the knife.

She closed her eyes, breath still, waiting for the bite of the knife into her throat.

There was a dull thud. Her eyes flew open as the knife fell from Hatcher's grip. Before she could get to her feet, Hatcher toppled over sideways, unconscious. Uncle Ken stood, ashen faced, blood running down his cheeks, a rock still gripped in his hand.

"It's over," he said, before he fell to his knees.

Barrett arrived at the Copper Creek Hospital within a half hour. As soon as he'd received Shelby's text, he'd called the cops and raced to the scene to find that both Shelby and her uncle had already been discovered by a passing officer, who had summoned an ambulance and got them to the hospital.

Barret's mind still spun with the information he'd heard from Larraby, that Joe Hatcher had been arrested at the scene and was on another floor of the hospital being treated for a head injury inflicted by Ken Arroyo as he defended his niece's life. Barrett forced himself not to run along the tiled hallways as he made his way to Shelby.

He found her pacing, arms hugged around herself. She looked over and saw him, stopping her endless laps around the waiting room. She didn't move, but tears streaked from her eyes. He didn't say a word, just pulled her close and let her cry onto his chest. When her tears were spent, he guided her to a chair.

"How is he?"

She sucked in a breath. "He was bleeding internally and he's in hypovolemic shock. They've given him a transfusion and medicines to help his heart beat more efficiently. They said they would have a better prognosis in the next twelve hours. He might be strong enough to recover, or his organs might shut down." Her voice wobbled.

"Okay," he said, squeezing her hand. "And how about you?"

"I'm okay." She laughed bitterly. "It's like Emmaline said, I must be invincible. Only the people around me get hurt."

The misery in her voice made him pull her closer. "It's over now."

Larraby approached, sinking into a chair next to them. "I'm glad you are okay. We'll keep your samples as evidence until we've cleared the scene, then you can have them back," he said. "May I ask how your uncle is?"

Shelby repeated the diagnosis, her voice shaky.

Larraby nodded. "We're all hoping he pulls through."

"But why did this happen?" she said. "Why did Hatcher risk everything to steal the samples? They could be worth nothing at all."

"I think I have an answer to that," he said. "He can't take the chance that the samples pave the way for excavation of the mine."

"Because he killed Charlie?"

"That might be part of it."

They both stared at Larraby.

He continued. "We found another way into the mine on Oscar's property and sent in a team with a dog. They found Charlie's body, just like you said—" he paused "—and another one down there."

Barrett gaped. "What? Whose?"

"The remains appear to be female. She was wearing a necklace with C.H. engraved on the back."

Shelby gasped. "Cora Hatcher? Joe's wife?"

"Looks like she's been dead about five years, right about the time he told everyone she left town." They fell into stunned silence for a few moments.

"Why Charlie, though?" Barrett said. "What did he have to do with Hatcher?"

"Nothing, except he was probably at the wrong place at the wrong time. He was getting close to discovering Cora's body with his exploring, so Hatcher killed him and covered up the body." Larraby tapped a finger on his notebook. "Hatcher might have figured he would go back and dispose of the remains more permanently at some point."

"Which would explain the red marks he left to point the way to the bodies," Shelby said. She shivered and Barrett rubbed her shoulders. "It's over now," he said again.

Shelby shook her head, exhaustion shadowing her face. "No, it's not. Emmaline's father is going to stay in prison for his whole life now because he murdered her mother. It's never going to be over for her." Her eyes flooded again. "And my uncle. What if he doesn't survive?"

Barrett took her hand and they stood. "Come on."

She allowed him to help her to her feet. "Where are we going?"

"To the chapel. We'll see you later, Larraby."

The officer gave a short nod before speaking into his radio.

They made their way to the empty chapel and linked hands to pray. Shelby clung to Barrett, hands shaking, while he prayed for Ken Arroyo. At first the words were forced, until something loosened inside him and he felt his hatred slipping away like a blanket of fog, dissipating in the warmth of the sunlight. When the prayer ended, he hung on to the feeling, marveling, grateful, awed.

They sat in silence, each lost in their own thoughts, as the time passed away. When Shelby began to droop, he led her back to the deserted waiting room where she lay down on an upholstered couch. He covered her with his jacket. She fought to stay awake.

"But what if the doctors come? If Uncle Ken wakes up?"

"I'll stay right here. I'll wake you if there's any change."

Her lovely green eyes fixed on his and her voice was very small. "I'm scared to be alone."

He knew what it cost her to admit it. "I'm here," he said, while he watched her slip into sleep.

Barrett felt caged by the confines of the waiting room. He wandered to the threshold of Ken Arroyo's room and then found himself standing at the man's bed. Ken's face was scratched and battered, lined with wrinkles too pronounced for a man of his age. Though he was a big guy, almost Barrett's height, the hospital bed and the crowded machinery dwarfed him.

There were no words to explain why Barrett laid his hand on Ken's forearm, just the urging of his soul. He closed his eyes. "I know…" he began, then his breath failed and he needed to take another one. "I know that you love your son as much as I loved my wife."

"Yes," came a croak of a reply.

Barrett's eyes flew open to see Ken Arroyo watching him, irises bright with some unnamed emotion.

"And…and I know that you tried to be a good father."

Ken didn't answer, but his chin quivered and a single tear ran down his cheek.

"I've been wrong to hang on to hatred," Barrett said. "I guess I need to ask for forgiveness as much as I need to offer it."

Slowly, Ken reached out until his shaking hand was inches from Barrett. Barrett grasped the cold fingers and he felt the hard stone of hatred dissolve in his heart. In Ken's eyes, Barrett saw that he, too, had moved toward a place of peace.

Barrett heard someone behind him and turned to find Shelby moving next to him, her own eyes streaming with tears, mouth trembling. She joined her hand to theirs, her crying twined with the soft sounds of the machinery.

Shelby awoke on the hard hospital couch, Barrett sitting quietly next to her. It took her a moment to realize that the previous day and long restless night had not been a dream. The most incredible part had really happened, her uncle had awakened, and he and Barrett had shared a divine moment of forgiveness.

Through the fatigue and worry, the thought circled light and airy in her heart. So what did it mean for her and Barrett, she wondered? But it was not the time to think about it.

Barrett's family had arrived in shifts throughout the previous day and all through the night, making sure she was never alone. Now, when it was Evie's turn, she sent Jack and Barrett off to fetch the Styrofoam container of soup that she had left in the truck.

"Piping hot. It's much better than the hospital cafeteria food, and I thought you might like some since you did not have dinner last night," she said. Then she cleared her throat. "Shelby, I am so sorry about all that's happened. I wish… I mean, I shouldn't have…"

Shelby gripped her hand. "You love your son. There's no need to apologize for anything."

Evie bit her lip and took a breath. "I want you to come to Christmas Eve dinner at the ranch. Your uncle, too, if he is released."

"That's a very kind offer but…"

Evie held up a palm. "It's not an offer, it's an invitation. I want you to be there, and so does our family."

Shelby blinked against the tears. "Thank you."

The doctor found them in the waiting room.

"He's improving steadily," she said. "I would venture to say he is going to make a complete recovery in the next week or so."

Shelby could not help but hug her around the shoulders.

The doctor laughed. "I wish I could deliver this

kind of news all the time. Now, why don't you go home for a bit?"

"No, I want to stay here."

"Your uncle is sleeping peacefully and there's no reason you can't pop home for a nap and a change of clothes."

Shelby looked down, realizing she was wearing the same ripped and stained jeans, though Evie had insisted she put on one of Barrett's flannel shirts.

"Go on, honey," Evie said as Barrett and Jack arrived with a paper sack and the container of soup. "Take the soup home and eat it. Jack and I will stay right here while Barrett drives you home. He'll pick you up whenever you're ready to return, since you seem to have trouble with vehicles."

Shelby laughed. "All right. Just for a little while. I want to be sure the horses are taken care of." She shot a look at Barrett. "Are you sure you don't mind?"

"Naw, I'm pretty sure Mama packed some Christmas cookies in this bag so I will take that in lieu of a taxicab fee."

She followed him to his truck, happy to sink down on the seat and watch the scenery go by. The soup container in the cup holder let off a cloud of savory scent. Her senses felt dull and slow with the shock of all that had happened, mostly that Joe Hatcher had killed his wife and Charlie, and almost added her, Barrett and Uncle Ken to the list.

Barrett scurried to open the door for her when

they arrived and she let him. "I want to make sure Zeke has been seeing to the horses before I allow myself that shower," she said.

They walked up the slope and down toward the stables. A figure stepped from the shadowed barn. At first she thought it was Zeke until they got closer.

"Emmaline," Shelby said, her heart breaking. "I am so sorry for everything that's happened."

"I'm not," Emmaline said, pulling a gun from behind her skirt and firing.

TWENTY-FOUR

The bullet creased a hot trail along Barrett's temple, hurling him to his back on the ground. He heard Shelby scream and drop to her knees beside him.

"Why did you do that?" Shelby panted. "Barrett," she whispered, fingers skimming his face as she tried to ascertain his injury.

"Diamond doesn't even know me anymore," Emmaline said. "My mother gave me that horse and now…"

Though his vision was blurred, Barrett could see Emmaline's face twisted into a mask of hatred. He would not have recognized her.

"You can have the horse," Shelby said. "Take her, just leave us alone."

Emmaline did not appear to hear. "My mother sold her, just like that, wanted to move away from here. She didn't care that I loved Diamond, loved Gold Bar. She never cared what I wanted. I hated her."

Barrett felt a sick sensation creep through the

pain in his head. "You…" he wanted to say, but the words wouldn't come.

"So…" Shelby started, then stopped. She sucked in a breath as she must have come to the same realization. "Oh, Emmaline. You killed your mother, didn't you?"

The girl didn't answer.

"And your father, he did all these things to keep us out of the mine…in order to protect you."

"I did some of it," she said proudly. "I'm handy with TNT and paint, and I've been snooping around the Thorns' property, keeping tabs on your activities. I am a good snooper. I knew Dad's idea to lock you in the trunk wouldn't be enough, so I had to take the reins, so to speak."

"Charlie," Barrett croaked in a desperate bid to keep her talking. "Why?"

"I didn't want to kill him," Emmaline said. "He was handsome and funny. I got to know him when I helped out at the inn sometimes. I didn't want to hurt him, but he kept on pushing deeper into the mine. I really did like him, but I couldn't let him find Mother so I got him to take me along, and one shot, that was all. It was peaceful."

Shelby gasped. "I can't believe this."

"Maybe you'll believe it when I shoot you," Emmaline said with a cunning smile. "Bullets are very convincing. I didn't want to hurt you at first either. I mean, I helped you escape the mine and all, just to keep you safe and Daddy out of trouble for his dumb practical joke, but see where that kindness got me."

"But you can't hide the truth anymore, Emmaline," Shelby said. "The bodies have been discovered now, Charlie and your mother."

"And Daddy has already confessed. He will stick to the story because he loves me. I am all he has, you know, since Mother is dead, but if you persist in analyzing the samples, eventually the mine will be fully excavated and there will be evidence found to incriminate me."

"What evidence?" Barrett said.

"I was angry. I painted messages on the tunnel walls sometimes, like I did at your uncle's house." She frowned. "It was stupid. I should have covered over them or moved the bodies, but I never got around to it."

"The police are investigating. They'll find your messages soon," Shelby said.

"No one will find them," she snapped, "unless your assaying causes mining to start up again, but I think when you disappear and are found dead eventually, your uncle will lose interest in his mining adventure."

Shelby's voice was high and taut. "How are you going to explain our murders?"

"I don't have to, but really, you're nosy, and nosy people get into trouble, don't they? Poor Barrett, getting mixed up with the likes of you. His wife was much better. She brought us Christmas cookies every year. It was a shame your cousin killed her. She didn't deserve to die, not like you."

Don't talk about my wife, Barrett wanted to say. *And Shelby doesn't deserve any of this*. He eased a little onto one side, grabbing a handful of gravel. Shelby squeezed his arm to show she'd noticed. She knew what they had to do.

"You don't have to do this," Shelby said, slowly standing. "We can explain it to the police. I am sure you didn't mean to kill her. It could have been an accident."

"No," Emmaline said, eyes blazing. "It was not an accident. My mother was a selfish shrew. My father fawned all over her like a puppy and she didn't care about him, or me. She sold the horses and told Daddy she was leaving us. It wasn't an accident," Emmaline snapped. "I shot her with this gun in the back of the head, just like I did to Charlie. Daddy has spent his whole life trying to cover it up, and now he's even gone to jail for it, so it's all up to me. You two are the only ones who know the truth."

She's insane, Barrett thought. His fingers tightened around the gravel. Without warning, Emmaline stomped down hard on his wrist. He grunted in pain, losing his grip on the bits of rock.

"If you think you're going to try something heroic, Mr. Thorn, you are making a mistake. Now, get up. We're going to walk to your truck and drive."

Shelby hooked an arm under his elbow and he

got unsteadily to his feet, blood dripping from his face onto his shirtfront. "Where?" he said.

"Somewhere remote, where you won't be found for a while. It will be fun watching them search for you."

They made their way toward the truck, Emmaline behind them, gun aimed. Once they were out of town, there would be a much smaller chance they would survive. The window of opportunity was narrowing.

Barrett squeezed Shelby's hand. Her fingers trembled in his. In that touch, he wanted to tell her so many things about how he'd changed since he met her, about what he'd learned deep down in his soul. Above all, he hoped she knew he would not give up fighting for her until his very last breath, and he had no intention of breathing his last to clear the way for Emmaline to cover up two murders.

"You drive," Emmaline said, prodding him in the back when they reached the vehicle.

"Can't," he said. "Double vision, thanks to your shot."

Shelby flicked him a worried look from the corner of her eye. Head turned away from Emmaline, he winked.

"You, then," she said to Shelby. Barrett handed her the keys. She dropped them and Emmaline cursed at her. While she bent to retrieve them, he yanked open the passenger door and started to climb in. There was only one thing he could use to save them. Praying, he grabbed the container. He had it in his hands, the soup still hot enough that the container was warm against his fingers. Whirling, he flung the soup into Emmaline's face.

She recoiled, raising her arms reflexively to her eyes, gun pointed at the sky. Shelby swept an ankle out and hooked Emmaline's legs. The gun went flying and Barrett pinned Emmaline down, turning her onto her stomach and holding her hands behind her back.

"Don't touch me," she hissed into the dirt. "Let me go."

"Happy to oblige as soon as the police arrive," he said, panting.

Shelby grabbed a coil of rope from the back of the truck and tied Emmaline's hands. Together, they knelt over Emmaline's prostrate form, breathing hard. Barrett still could not quite believe that the young girl they held had killed her own mother and an innocent college student.

And nearly killed them both as well, he reminded himself. Shelby shivered next to him and he figured she was running through those chilling thoughts, as well.

"All kinds of crazy?" she said, a sliver of a smile on her face.

"That's exactly what I was about to say."

Christmas Eve morning, Shelby was at her uncle's side, prodding him to eat from a dish of applesauce while she explained what had happened at the ranch. He was still pale, weak, but improving at a steady rate, according to the doctors. She had stopped in the chapel on her way to his room to thank God for her uncle's deliverance and theirs. The world had spun out of control for so long, she hardly knew what to do with herself now that He'd put it back in order.

Barrett had not wanted her to spend the night alone at her uncle's and she suspected he might have even slept in his truck outside, but she did not feel frightened anymore. Emmaline, poor twisted girl, was in custody and there would be no more threats to Shelby or her uncle. Shelby had wrapped up in her blankets, cried, prayed, thought about her mother, about Barrett and her future and prayed some more, sleeping intermittently until morning dawned.

With effort, she brought her mind back to the present. "When the police release my samples, I'll get them analyzed as quickly as I can."

Uncle Ken pushed the applesauce aside. "No need."

"What?"

"I'm okay, for a while, like I said, and it doesn't feel right to pry open that mine anytime soon. Too much grief contained in those tunnels for my taste."

She felt her eyes well up again. "Charlie's parents will arrive soon to take home his remains."

Uncle Ken sighed. "That's good. Some closure."

He patted her hand. "So what are your Christmas Eve plans?"

"I'm going to stay here with you. I'll see if I can smuggle in some cookies or something."

"Not necessary. Evie Thorn called just before you arrived to say she and Tom will be here precisely at noon to deliver me a Christmas luncheon that will fill me to the rafters."

Shelby gaped. "And you're...well, you're okay with that?"

He was quiet a moment. "Let's just say I've learned a few things recently. It will take time," he said, eyes damp, "but I want things to be different."

She blinked back her own tears and kissed him on the cheek. "I'm so glad, Uncle Ken."

"So," he said, after clearing his throat, "you are to attend the Christmas Eve gathering at the Gold Bar Ranch tonight, Shelby, no arguments."

"I'm not going to leave you here alone."

"Trust me, after Evie's lunch I think I will be napping the day away. Nothing sounds better to me than a night of uninterrupted sleep. Please," he said, catching her hand, "I want you to go."

It doesn't seem right, she wanted to say, but she found to her surprise that it did. Spending Christmas Eve with Barrett was the only thing her heart craved. She did not know where things stood between them, but she knew she had to see him again.

"If you're sure," she said.

He pulled her hand to his mouth and kissed her knuckles. "I'm sure. Go."

On the way down in the elevator, she made plans. First, a call to her mother to tell her caregivers she'd be coming for a visit soon. Then a proper shower and an attempt to make herself presentable. And one very important stop in town...

The Christmas Eve service at the church was packed as usual. Everyone greeted Barrett with extra hearty hugs that made his ribs throb and he heard "I just can't believe it" more times than he could count. He was still having trouble believing it himself.

And further, he could not stop wondering about Shelby, where she was and if he had done the right thing on his afternoon errand after his mother confirmed that Shelby would likely be coming to Christmas Eve at the ranch. Barrett was not prone to indecision, but now his stomach felt tight.

As the choir sang the last Christmas carol, his eye caught a glimpse of brown glossy hair pulled into a soft pile. Shelby? He strained to see, but he was caught up in the throng of churchgoers filing down the aisle. Most of them would be heading to the ranch directly. His mother tugged on his arm.

"Come on, Barrett. We've got mouths to feed."

"Right behind you, Mama." He strained to look for Shelby but there was no sign of her.

At the ranch, he was immediately engulfed by

his duties. The long wooden tables he'd constructed were covered and set with pine garlands and flickering lanterns. He activated the tall heat lamps and his father threw more wood into the crackling fire pit. Jack stood at the fence, armed with carrots that he dispensed for the children to offer the horses that stood expectantly on the other side. Owen poured endless cups of cider and hot coffee. It was good to see him smiling.

It seemed like this year the eight-foot tree standing near the front porch sparkled with more lights than in recent memory, and the buffet table was jammed with an unbelievable assortment of offerings, everything from roast turkey to mashed potatoes, cranberry relish and plates of his mother's famous stuffing.

Keegan was posted at the dessert table, ostensibly to keep the kids from raiding it before supper, but Barrett saw his youngest brother sneaking cookies to the kids and nibbling on them himself. Barrett chuckled. Tonight would be a night of rejoicing, finishing up with a rousing family game time and a midnight prayer.

Thorn family Christmases. He'd taken them for granted. The last four years he'd been so steeped in grief, in hatred, that Christmases had come and gone in a meaningless parade. Bree would have tugged on his earlobe and told him not to waste a minute being regretful on Christmas Eve. Bree had always relished the life God had given her, and Barrett was going to try to do the same.

"I'll always love you, Bree," he whispered, looking up at the spangle of stars. A feeling of peace filled his soul.

But he had not yet seen Shelby. What if she did not come?

"Is it okay to start with dessert and work my way backward?"

He spun on his heel and found Shelby standing there, clutching a box. Her hair was piled up like he'd noticed in church and she wore a red sweater and a white scarf.

"Pretty as a Christmas present," he murmured.

She smiled, looking away. "Speaking of presents…" She handed him the wrapped box.

"You didn't have to get me a gift," he said.

"Yes, I did. Open it."

He tore off the paper and pulled off the lid. Inside was a cowboy hat, sturdy and unadorned.

"I know it's not as good as your favorite hat that you lost in the mine," she said.

He clapped it on his head. "It'll be perfect, once I beat it up a little. Thank you."

She laughed. "Glad I didn't get the one with rhinestones on the side."

He chuckled. "Good call. I, uh… I got something for you, too."

He took her hand and led her over to the glistening Christmas tree. From underneath it, he took a tissue-wrapped package. "Hope you like it."

With nerves zinging, he watched her open it. Her laughter drifted through the air like snowflakes. "A jar of homemade pickles," she cried. "I'm going to keep them forever, unopened, to remind me of you."

He pointed to the ribbon around the edge. "Maybe, um, you could keep that instead."

Eyes wide, she untied the ribbon and slid off the gold ring. "Barrett?"

"It's an engagement ring." He could hardly swallow. "I mean, if you want it to be."

She stared at him, the ring clutched between her fingers.

"I love you, Shelby," he said. "You brought my heart back to beating and you helped me see that I was wasting my life on hatred."

She cocked her head, her expression...puzzled? Confused? *Upset?* he thought with a trickle of fear.

"I thought I didn't have any more right to experience joy after Bree, but being with you has changed all that. I want you to be in my life."

"But you almost died because of me."

"No," he said quietly. "It's the opposite. You taught me how to live again."

Tears glimmered on the edges of her thick lashes. Tears of joy, he told himself stubbornly as he eased down to one knee, slid off his hat and took the ring from her hands.

"Will you marry me, Shelby?"

Her mouth opened in a circle of surprise, but she did not speak one reassuring syllable.

He cleared his throat. "If it feels rushed, we can have a long engagement, as long as you want. I know you want to set up your own assayer's office, and there's your mother to think about. I don't want you to give up anything, so if you need time, I understand, but tell me that you want a future with me." He sucked in a breath. "I'm just a simple cowboy, and I know that's not much to offer, but I promise I will love you forever, Shelby. Tell me that you love me, too."

The wind carried the sounds of Christmas music and laughter. Maybe he'd been wrong, misread her heart and mistakenly equated her feelings with his. Suddenly he felt cold, foolish. He got to his feet.

"I, uh..."

She leaped into his arms. Astonished, he lifted her off her feet as she pressed her face to his.

"You know what, Barrett Thorn?" she said, cheeks rosy and eyes glittering.

"What?" he breathed, experiencing an upwelling of hope.

"I would be honored to be the wife of a simple, pickle-making cowboy. I love you."

Jubilation filled his soul and he knew Bree would be happy, too, that he had found another remarkable woman to love. He kissed Shelby long and slow.

She giggled. "Are you sure you're going to be

able to handle it when I beat you at checkers during family game night, cowboy?"

"I'll never surrender," he said, laughing. Then he swept her closer and kissed her properly.

Cowboy-style.

* * * * *

If you enjoyed
COWBOY CHRISTMAS GUARDIAN,
look for these other books
by Dana Mentink.

DANGEROUS TIDINGS
SEASIDE SECRETS
ABDUCTED
DANGEROUS TESTIMONY

Dear Reader,

What is it about cowboy heroes? There's a mystique about the hardworking cowboy, the tough, honorable, God-fearing man who isn't afraid to speak the truth or fight for his family honor. I am thrilled to bring you this new series featuring the Thorn family—four brothers who will face any danger to protect their beloved Gold Bar Ranch and the women whom they will come to love along the way.

In this first installment in the series, Barrett Thorn must come face-to-face with his inability to forgive those who were responsible for the death of his wife. It's a struggle for a man with a deep faith, who knows what God wants from him. In the course of the novel, he'll meet a woman who challenges his beliefs and his feelings, as they both seek to solve a mystery and stay alive.

Thank you for coming on this new journey into cowboy country! I hope you will enjoy riding along with me. As always, I am blessed to hear from my readers. You can contact me via my website at www.danamentink.com and there is also a physical address there if you'd like to write. God bless you, my friends, and welcome to Gold Country!

Sincerely,
Dana Mentink

Get 2 Free Books,
Plus 2 Free Gifts—
just for trying the
Reader Service!

YES! Please send me 2 FREE Love Inspired® Romance novels and my 2 FREE mystery gifts (gifts are worth about $10 retail). After receiving them, if I don't wish to receive any more books, I can return the shipping statement marked "cancel." If I don't cancel, I will receive 6 brand-new novels every month and be billed just $5.24 for the regular-print edition or $5.74 each for the larger-print edition in the U.S., or $5.74 each for the regular-print edition or $6.24 each for the larger-print edition in Canada. That's a saving of at least 13% off the cover price. It's quite a bargain! Shipping and handling is just 50¢ per book in the U.S. and 75¢ per book in Canada.* I understand that accepting the 2 free books and gifts places me under no obligation to buy anything. I can always return a shipment and cancel at any time. The free books and gifts are mine to keep no matter what I decide.

Please check one:
- ☐ Love Inspired Romance Regular-Print (105/305 IDN GLWW)
- ☐ Love Inspired Romance Larger-Print (122/322 IDN GLWW)

Name _____ (PLEASE PRINT)

Address _____ Apt. #

City _____ State/Province _____ Zip/Postal Code

Signature (if under 18, a parent or guardian must sign)

Mail to the **Reader Service:**
IN U.S.A.: P.O. Box 1341, Buffalo, NY 14240-8531
IN CANADA: P.O. Box 603, Fort Erie, Ontario L2A 5X3

Want to try two free books from another line?
Call 1-800-873-8635 today or visit www.ReaderService.com.

*Terms and prices subject to change without notice. Prices do not include applicable taxes. Sales tax applicable in N.Y. Canadian residents will be charged applicable taxes. Offer not valid in Quebec. This offer is limited to one order per household. Books received may not be as shown. Not valid for current subscribers to Love Inspired Romance books. All orders subject to approval. Credit or debit balances in a customer's account(s) may be offset by any other outstanding balance owed by or to the customer. Please allow 4 to 6 weeks for delivery. Offer available while quantities last.

Your Privacy—The Reader Service is committed to protecting your privacy. Our Privacy Policy is available online at www.ReaderService.com or upon request from the Reader Service.

We make a portion of our mailing list available to reputable third parties that offer products we believe may interest you. If you prefer that we not exchange your name with third parties, or if you wish to clarify or modify your communication preferences, please visit us at www.ReaderService.com/consumerchoice or write to us at Reader Service Preference Service, P.O. Box 9062, Buffalo, NY 14240-9062. Include your complete name and address.

LI17R2

Get 2 Free Books,
Plus 2 Free Gifts —
just for trying the
Reader Service!

READERSERVICE.COM

Manage your account online!

- Review your order history
- Manage your payments
- Update your address

> **We've designed the Reader Service website just for you.**

Enjoy all the features!

- Discover new series available to you, and read excerpts from any series.
- Respond to mailings and special monthly offers.
- Browse the Bonus Bucks catalog and online-only exculsives.
- Share your feedback.

Visit us at:

ReaderService.com